Rangeland Justice

When Jack Just, weary from long days on the trail, rides into an isolated cattle town on the Texas Panhandle, he discovers that the greedy and powerful Clovis Blacklake has the whole town in his pocket.

But when Jack discovers that Blacklake has cheated the town's most downtrodden inhabitant out of his rightful property, he decides to make a stand.

It takes a real man to fight the ruthless Blacklake and when Jack does, the tables finally begin to turn. . . .

Rangeland Justice

Rob Hill

A Black Horse Western

ROBERT HALE · LONDON

© Rob Hill 2010
First published in Great Britain 2010

ISBN 978-0-7090-8936-0

Robert Hale Limited
Clerkenwell House
Clerkenwell Green
London EC1R 0HT

www.halebooks.com

Typeset by
Derek Doyle & Associates, Shaw Heath
Printed and bound in Great Britain by
CPI Antony Rowe, Chippenham and Eastbourne

To Val and Joss

1

The lone rider dismounted and gently lifted the baby calf down from his saddle. The calf teetered on unsteady legs, looked anxiously about him and took a few faltering steps. The rider spoke to him softly and patted him on the flank, staying close in case the animal should fall. He unhitched his canteen from the saddle, poured water into a tin bowl for the calf and encouraged him to drink. He poured more water for his horse, a handsome bay, and for the packmule, which followed behind loaded with a heavy canvas toolbag and a pack tied in oilcloth. The rider was Jack Just. The mule carried everything he owned in the world.

The ground here sloped down off a high ridge on to a vast plain below. It had been cut up by herds of longhorns and baked hard by the sun. This was the cattle trail north. Jack took in the view. He could see a town a few miles out on the plain. It didn't look much from here, just two rows of wooden buildings facing each other across a dusty street. It was typical of the cattle towns which had sprung up on the Texas panhandle since the war. Maybe, Jack thought, this would be somewhere he could stay awhile.

South of the town a cattle ranch sprawled across the plain. There was a huge ranch house, stables, workshops and row after row of cattle pens. Judging by the clouds of dust being kicked up, the cowboys were cutting the herd, ready for the spring drive. A mile to the west, at the foot of the ridge, there was a derelict homestead beside a dry creek. A cowboy was riding over the plain below him. Likely he was from the ranch, Jack thought, chasing up strays.

Down in the town, Sheriff Nathan 'Bull' Brown was staking out the saloon right across the street from his office window. He saw young Clem Hutchings, the champion roper from the Diamondback Ranch, slip inside, darting anxious glances over his shoulder, afraid he was being followed. Bull waited, never taking his eyes off the saloon door. His hand instinctively rested on the handle of the Remington in his holster.

After a few minutes, the Johnson brothers, rushed into the sheriff's office. Silas and Bill Johnson were both sworn deputies. They worked in their father's hardware store down the street and were on call to assist the town's lawman whenever he needed them. They were both tall, stringy, mean-eyed men. They already had money from their parents' store and their promotion to deputies gave them power in the town. They just had to keep on the right side of Bull Brown.

'You sent for us, Sheriff?' Silas burst out, breathless from running up the street.

'There's a punk cowhand in the saloon needs to be

taught a lesson,' Bull said, still watching at the window. 'Ain't showed respect for the law and order in the town and been creating a disturbance. Name's Clem Hutchings.'

Silas and Bill Johnson looked at each other uncertainly. 'Clem from the Diamondback?' queried Silas.

'You heard me,' snarled Bull. 'You boys deal with it. And I don't want no paperwork.'

'You want us to arrest him, Sheriff?' Bill said, not catching on. 'Was he drunk or somethin'?'

Bull rounded on him, the colour rising up his thick neck. 'You want to stay a deputy? I told you, I don't want no paperwork.'

'OK, Sheriff,' Silas said. 'We understand. We'll wait till there's no one about.'

Inside the saloon Charlie, the bartender, was chatting to Hank, Guthrie and Clem, cowboys from the Diamondback Ranch, while he polished the glasses. Charlie had arrived on the panhandle just as the first buildings of the town were going up, the year the war ended. He had begun to work for Clovis Blacklake, proprietor of the Diamondback, the only employer in the area. Blacklake took to Charlie because of the calm and efficient way he had of dealing with things. When the saloon was built, he installed Charlie to run it for him.

The young cowhands liked nothing better than to listen to Charlie's stories about the old days. In particular, they relished his gossip about Blacklake, their employer, and about Bull Brown, the sheriff.

'How comes a guy like that gets to be sheriff?' Clem said.

9

'Easy. He used to be foreman at the Diamondback, where you boys are workin'. When the war was going on, all the herds got mixed up all over the panhandle. There was no one to look after 'em. They jus' wandered every which way. Some of 'em was branded, some of 'em wasn't. When they came home from the army, your boss, Mr Blacklake and Bull Brown rounded up whatever cattle they could get their hands on, whoever it belonged to, an' drove 'em down to the market in New Orleans. They did four drives in two years. They were hard workin' sonsabitches in them days. Blacklake made a fortune. Bull was his sidekick. When Blacklake began to build the town, he made Bull sheriff. That way he'd own everything and Bull would control it for him too.'

The cowboys were fascinated.

Charlie reflected. 'Mr Blacklake is a real good businessman. He has a way of makin' every deal turn out so he's the winner. There was one time in Missouri when Blacklake sold five hundred head to a rancher, then he drove 'em round the hill and sold 'em to him again. Damnedest thing I ever heard. Fella thought he'd bought a thousand head but he just bought the same five hundred twice. Paid Blacklake for a thousand head too.'

'Damn,' Clem said. 'High and mighty Clovis Blacklake, boss of the biggest ranch on the panhandle started out as a cheat and a cattle thief. Well, if that don't take the rag.'

'Yeah. I'll tell you somthin' else too,' Charlie said, relishing the gossip. 'You know Blacklake got a sister?'

'Lemonade Lil,' Hank grinned.

'Don't you let Blacklake hear you call her that or you'll wake up on the high plains without any horse,' Charlie

10

said quickly. 'Adela, her name is. She's the schoolteacher and the town nurse, leastways the nearest we've got to one. Anyway, old Bull Brown is pretty sweet on Adela. He's bin tryin' to make a mash on her for a long time. He's been takin' her bunches of flowers and she's been bakin' him apple pie for a year or more.'

'Always had Bull down as a whores-and-whiskey kinda guy.' Clem grinned. 'I'd like to see him holdin' a bunch of flowers.'

The others laughed.

'You kin laugh,' Charlie said seriously. 'But you better be careful, Clem. You overstepped the mark yesterday. You started makin' remarks about likin' lemonade an' apple pie an' such when Bull was in here. Ol' Bull ain't so bright as sunshine but he caught on to what you were doin' all right. I kin tell you, he don't take kindly to bein' teased at all. 'Specially by a young fella like you.'

Clem looked anxious. 'I didn't mean nothin' by it. You all know that.' He looked to the others for support. 'Anyways, I ain't gonna stay around. I'm goin' back out to the ranch.'

Two guys were sitting in the shadows round the side of the saloon and one of them called Clem over as he passed. 'Hey, Mister. You the guy won the lassoing competition in Dodge City a few months back?' Clem hesitated and smiled at the flattery. As he turned towards them, Silas's fist exploded into his face and broke his nose.

Clem reeled backwards, his hand instinctively covering his face. Bill emerged from the shadows and hauled the whimpering Clem into the gap between the buildings, out

11

of sight of the street. Clem was still staggering, dazed and in pain with blood gushing down his face and shirt as Bill punched him hard in the kidneys and then kicked his legs from under him. Clem landed on his back in the dust, his hands still trying to protect his broken nose.

Silas leaned over him. 'Listen cowboy. We don' like you causin' trouble here. We don' like you disrespectin' folks in our town. We don' like you givin' the sheriff none o' your lip. Fact is, we plain don' like you. . . .' With that he gave Clem a mighty kick in the stomach which knocked most of the breath out of him. Bill joined in, kicking him in the back and side and stamping on his legs with the heel of his boot. All Clem could do was to draw himself in as tight as he could and cover his head with his arms while the kicking continued. Eventually his moaning and pleas for mercy stopped and he made no movement. Silas and Bill looked down at their handiwork and grinned at each other. 'Two 'gainst one,' sneered Bill. 'Ain't fair, is it?'

Across the street Sheriff Bull Brown had watched the whole thing from his office window. He smiled with grim satisfaction when he saw Clem's body lying still. Those Johnson boys were good, he thought. Just the kind of deputies he needed.

Bull adjusted his hat and straightened his tie in the small mirror which hung on a nail beside the door. He stepped out into the sunlight, waved briefly to Silas and Bill across the street and strode off in the opposite direction.

'Think he saw?' Bill asked Silas excitedly.

'Hell, yeah. I'll bet he was watchin' outa his window all

the time. Old Bull wouldn't miss a thing like that.' Silas laughed. 'Ain't nothin' he likes better.'

There was no one about as Jack rode into town. Everyone was indoors taking refuge from the afternoon heat. The place looked prosperous enough, he thought. The timber buildings were new. It was typical of these cattle towns. Men had grown rich quickly here since the war ended. There was a lumber yard stacked high with planed pine next to the stables, ready to be used for more construction. He should be able to find carpentry work here.

Main Street was closed. The blinds were drawn across the windows of Johnson's Hardware and, next door, the bank was shut. There was no movement in the sheriff's office and the grocery store was quiet. The sun had bleached the dusty street almost white. The heat reflecting off the ground slapped Jack in the face and stung his eyes. He headed for the saloon to get into the shade and to ask about somewhere to stay.

Two blocks down from where he was, a figure suddenly reeled out from the narrow yard between the saloon and the gunsmith's. The cowboy lurched from side to side, hardly able to walk. 'Drunk in the afternoon.' Jack smiled to himself. 'Getting set up for that long, dry cattle drive.' After a helpless stagger, which showed the man was unable to walk in a straight line, the cowboy collapsed on to his knees while holding both hands over his face. As Jack approached he realized that the front of the cowboy's shirt was soaked in blood and his hands and face were splashed with it. Jack immediately leapt off his horse and ran towards him.

Jack gently lifted the man's hands away from his face so he could inspect the damage. His nose was cut, broken and swelling like an overripe plum. Jack noticed the tears in his shirt and pants. He helped the young cowboy to his feet. 'You sure ain't everybody's friend, pal,' he said. 'Got to get some ice on that nose of yours afore it gets to be as big as the rest of your head.' The young man's eyes began to close as he sank out of consciousness again.

Hank and Guthrie, the cowboys at the bar, recoiled, horrified, when Jack shouldered his way through the saloon doors with Clem in his arms. Only fifteen minutes ago they had been sitting with him, listening to Charlie. Jack laid Clem down gently on the bar. A ginger tomcat, which had been basking in a pool of sunlight, skittered away in alarm.

Guthrie recognized Jack from meeting him up on the ridge the previous day.

'Hey, mister. You're the guy found the calf, when I was out lookin' for strays.'

'Ice,' Jack said.

'Ain't got no ice,' Charlie said. 'Damn wish we had too. Got a rag soaked in water is all.' He dipped the cloth he used for wiping the glasses into a bowl of water behind the bar and handed it to Jack. Jack put it in Clem's hand and guided his hand to the middle of his face. Clem held the cloth obediently.

'Reckon Bull Brown caught up with him,' Charlie said. 'I told 'im ol' Bull ain't got much of a sense of humour when it comes to bein' teased.' He leaned over Clem.

14

'Can you hear me? Who did this? Bull Brown?' Clem groaned and shook his head slightly. Every movement pained him.

'He says it ain't,' Hank said excitedly. 'He says it ain't Bull. Damn. Who was it, Clem? We'll get 'im. We'll tear his head off.'

Clem tried to answer, but his words came out as a moan from his swollen mouth. He raised his hand slowly and held up two fingers.

'Two?' queried Guthrie. 'Is he telling us there were two of them?'

Clem moaned in agreement.

'Yes he is, damnit,' said Hank. 'Bull and someone else? Is that what you're tellin' us?'

Clem attempted to shake his head.

'Best get 'im down to Miss Adela's at the school house. She'll patch him up. Won't get no sense out of him till he's patched up,' Charlie said. 'I don' want him bleedin' all over my bar anyways.'

'Which way's that?' Jack asked.

'End of the street,' Charlie said. 'You can't miss it. Come back when you've finished. We don't see many new faces round here.'

'Can you walk?' Jack said to Clem. Clem nodded. Jack helped him down off the bar and steadied him. He put one arm round Clem and led him out of the saloon in the direction of the schoolhouse. The other cowboys followed.

'Wouldn't want to fight no blowhard like Bull,' Guthrie said. 'He looks like he could kick off good an' proper and wouldn't know when to stop.'

'Clem said it weren't Bull,' Hank said.

' 'Course it was. Who else woulda done that? Clem don't have no beef with no one. Only Bull can't take a joke.'

2

At the other end of Main Street stood the schoolhouse. It was a square white-painted building, the only building on the dusty street to be fronted by a garden and a picket fence. An iron bell hung to one side of the door. Inside, there was one large room which contained four neat rows of low desks and benches.

A woman sat beside a little boy at one of the children's desks. The boy was slowly and deliberately drawing the letters of the alphabet in chalk on a piece of slate the size of a roof shingle. When he'd used up the space, he wiped the slate clean with the sleeve of his shirt. Throughout this slow and deliberate process, the woman made encouraging noises and complimented the boy on the way he held the chalk and the shape of his letters.

The woman was Adela Blacklake, the schoolteacher, sister of Clovis Blacklake, owner of the Diamondback Ranch. Her manner with the boy was kindly and encouraging like a favourite aunt. She peered closely at his work through her thick spectacles and, being tall, sat with obvious discomfort at the child's desk. The boy was

Zachariah Johnson, brother of Silas and Bill, the town deputies. He liked Miss Blacklake because she often gave him candy, but hated writing his letters, which she had made him repeat many times.

'Well,' said Miss Blacklake when Zachariah at last arrived at Z. 'Very good, Zachariah. 'You wrote nice and big so even my poor old eyes could see your work and you made it through the whole alphabet without me having to tell you one single letter.'

'Except Q,' said Zachariah, honestly.

'No one minds about Q,' said Miss Blacklake in a confidential whisper. 'You're an excellent student. Now off you go and tell your folks I said so. Your pa will be wantin' you to sweep the store. I have a visitor comin' and I know he is very partial to apple pie, so I best get busy.'

'Thank you, Miss Blacklake,' Zachariah said cheerfully and skipped out of the schoolroom. At the door, he turned. 'Who's your visitor comin', Miss Blacklake?'

Adela laughed. 'Well if you must know, Zachariah, Mr Nathan Brown will be calling on me this evening. He's a friend of mine.'

'Bull Brown, the sheriff?' yelled Zachariah. 'Wow! Just wait till I tell Silas and Bill. Them's my brothers. They're old Bull's deputies! 'Bye, Miss Blacklake.'

Adela Blacklake wiped Zachariah's slate for him and put it on the pile on her desk. His brothers, Silas and Bill, had sat at these desks, as had all the children who had grown up in the town. Adela had taught them their letters and their numbers. They had basked in her encouraging smile in return.

Just as Zachariah left, Jack pushed through the door,

helping Clem along. Bill and Guthrie were right behind them. Adela, who had seen this kind of thing many times before, ushered Jack straight through the schoolroom into her parlour at the back. She told Clem to lie down on the chaise longue. The cowboys stood anxiously staring at their friend, turning their hats awkwardly in their hands. Adela gently moved Clem's hand, which held the blood-soaked rag, away from his face.

She inspected closely the wide, jagged cut across his swollen nose. 'You poor boy' she said softly. 'It doesn't look pretty but it'll heal. At least the wound's clean.' Then she added with gentle irony, 'I suppose you walked into a door.'

Clem gave a faint, painful smile. 'Yes, ma'am.'

Adela disappeared into the kitchen and came out a moment later with a white cloth and a basin of water. She proceeded to gently dab all the dried blood from Clem's bruised face. At Adela's instruction, Jack held Clem's head still between his two powerful hands while she wrapped scraps of cotton cloth around a series of matchsticks and pulled out clots of blood from his nostrils. Clem's eyes were closed through all this, as he tried not to flinch against the jags of pain in his face. The cowboys watched in awe.

'Wish I had one of these I could give you,' Adela said as she unbuttoned Clem's shirt to inspect the bruises on his chest. 'This one's torn to ribbons.' Again she peered closely through her thick spectacles at the flaming pink and purple marks which covered his ribcage. 'Does it hurt when you breathe?' she asked kindly.

'Not too bad, ma'am,' Clem said. 'Is jus' sore is all.'

19

'Well that's good. Maybe you haven't broken any ribs. I can't be sure. You just lie there easy for now. That door surely did a good job on you.'

Clem tried to smile.

Adela turned to the others. 'Have you boys got enough money between you to buy him another shirt? Even if I could see well enough to thread a needle, this one's past repairing.'

The cowboys shuffled with embarrassment. 'No ma'am, we ain't. We don't get paid till the end of the drive.'

Adela felt in the purse which was clipped to the waistband of her skirt and produced a silver dollar. 'You go down the street to Johnson's Hardware and see Mrs. Johnson. You tell her that Adela Blacklake sent you and you want a shirt for your friend here and some change for me. I know she keeps shirts in there. She has them sent down on the wagon from Dodge City.'

The cowboys hesitated. 'Go on, take it.' She thrust the dollar into Guthrie's hand. 'Make sure you tell her it's for me.' The pair seemed rooted to the spot. Being unused to generosity, they hardly knew how to react. 'It's all right,' Adela said, sensing their unease, 'he can pay me back after the drive.' Jack silently noted her command of the situation. The cowboys mumbled 'Thank you ma'am' and left for the store.

'There's nothing else I can do for him,' Adela said to Jack. 'He's just got to rest now. If he's broken any ribs, he won't be going on the cattle drive, that's for sure. We should know by morning. Are you working out at the Diamondback too?'

'Got into town today,' Jack said. 'Name's Jack Just.'

'Well,' Adela said, 'I'm Adela Blacklake. It was good of you to bring that boy up here. I don't suppose those others would have, by themselves.' She smiled. 'And what brings you to this part of the panhandle, Mr Just, if you're not working at the Diamondback?'

'I'm lookin' for a place. Somewhere to settle down for a while. I been ridin' for a livin'. It feels like now's the right time for me to stay in one place.'

'And where did you do this riding, Mr Just?' Adela smiled pleasantly at him.

'Missouri, east of Fort Scott mostly. That's where I grew up. My pappy worked on a ranch up there, so I kinda grew up around horses. When the war came, I was fourteen, and because I could ride good they took me on as a messenger with the Virginia Cavalry. Didn't see home for five years. When I got back, there wasn't nothing left . . .' Jack paused, 'so there was nothing to stay for. I headed west towards the territories. Most of the jobs I got seemed to involve ridin' or shootin' or both. Protectin' sheep and cattle mainly, shootin' coyotes an' such. Either that or carpentry work. I like fixin' things.'

'The war was a terrible time for all of us,' Adela said. 'I only saw my brother twice in three years. His business collapsed. He had to work day and night to rebuild it when he came home in sixty-five. Well, if you're not a cattleman, you won't find any place to settle down round here.'

'I passed an old homestead on the way in. Looks like it needs some repairin'.'

'That's the old mission,' Adela said. 'My friend Mary was the pastor's wife out there. But she died from the

21

influenza. They both did. We had a terrible epidemic three years ago. Mary and Joe were good people. They built the mission to bring the love of Jesus to the Comanche. They brought up a little Comanche boy as if he were their own. He was given to them in a basket, so they called him Moses.'

'The Comanche gave away a child?' Jack asked.

'His hand was withered from birth, poor Moses,' Adela continued. 'I guess the Comanche didn't want him. Mary and Pastor Joe brought him up as a Christian. He was a sweet boy. After they died and the creek dried up my brother let him work in the livery stable.' She smiled. 'My brother is a good man, Mr Just, he built the town and aims to look after its people. That's what he says. He built the school, you know. If he hadn't I don't suppose anyone here would be able to read.'

Adela seemed thoughtful, as if she were explaining things to herself, rather than describing them to Jack. Jack listened calmly, letting her speak.

'I suppose it's worked out for the best, if dear Mary and the pastor can't be with us. Moses has work and somewhere to live and Clovis has been able to open up a new cattle route. He runs the herd through the old mission property now. It saves nearly fifteen miles. The cattle had to be driven round the edge of the bluff before. When the pastor was alive, he would never let Clovis drive the herd through. He used to say: "If you drive the cattle through, you drive the Comanche away." I never saw why that should have been true at all. I persuaded Mary to talk to him, but he wouldn't agree. He may have been a man of God but he was stubborn as you like. Anyway, I don't know what I'm telling you all that for.'

Adela pulled herself together. 'Now, Mr Just, I have a room out back which I sometimes let to travellers passing through. You would be welcome to it if you haven't made other plans. But I think we ought to let this young man have a bed tonight. He shouldn't try to ride out to the Diamondback now. If his ribs are all intact in the morning, he'll be on his way and you can take the room. I should like you to help me get him to the bed, though, before you leave.'

'Surely,' Jack said. 'Then I'd best get my horse down to the livery stable.'

As Jack was unhitching his horse from the rail in front of the saloon, Charlie called him inside.

'Mighty nice of you to take Clem up to Adela's. How is he?'

'Oh, he'll be seein' stars for a while, then I guess he'll be all right. Somebody sure don't like him, though.'

Clem looked serious for a moment. Then he ushered Jack inside and led him to the bar.

'Seen these?' He indicated the pile of rolled advertising posters on the bar.

'Saw one up by the door as I came in,' Jack said. 'Can't say I read it though.'

Charlie unrolled one of the posters to show Jack. It said 'Undefeated Chinaman Prizefighter Lee Yoo will take on all comers. Lazy Dog Saloon Saturday 18 May 1872, 9 p.m. Hundred-dollar purse. Gloves worn. No bare knuckle. Admission 25c. Fight arranged courtesy of Mr Clovis Blacklake, Diamondback Ranch.'

'That's this Saturday,' Charlie said excitedly. 'Everyone's lookin' forward to it, sure as hell. We're gonna have the fight right in here. Mr Blacklake is puttin' up the hundred-dollar purse. It's celebratin' the seventh cattle drive north from the Diamondback. Guys'll come from all over.'

'Who's gonna take the Chinaman on?' Jack asked.

'Oh there'll be some fool cattleman who thinks he can get the bulge on him and win an easy hundred bucks. Then there'll be another one who thinks that the Chinaman will be weakened by the first guy, and he'll stand a chance that way. Then there'll be another one from somewhere. It'll be a bang-up night.' He passed a glass of beer over the bar to Jack.

The saloon door opened and Bull Brown stepped in. He paused for a moment to let his eyes adjust to the shadows after the bright sunlight outside. He strode straight up to the bar and glared fiercely at Jack. 'Saw your horse and mule tethered. Name's Nate Brown, but everyone calls me Bull on account of my reputation as a prizefighter when I was younger. I'm sheriff here.' He indicated his tin star.

'Jack Just.' Jack extended his hand but Bull ignored it.

'What's your business here, mister? This here's a cattle town and you don't look like no cattleman.'

'Been moving south for a while,' Jack said, 'lookin' for a place to put down some roots. Lookin' for carpentry work too. Anythin' that means I don't have to live in the saddle.'

'Well, you won't find no place around here if you ain't a cattleman,' Bull said. 'We had a few drifters pass through here. But none of 'em stayed. I'm reckonin' you won't neither.'

'Yeah?' Jack said evenly.

Bull turned to Charlie. 'Anyone put their names forward for fightin' the Chinaman?'

'Not yet.' Charlie grinned. He started to polish glasses and line them up behind the bar.

'You shoulda seen me ten years ago,' continued the sheriff. 'I broke a man's jaw once. He was twice my size. There was a fifty-dollar purse that night. I cracked my head round so hard, I caught him on the jaw. Fractured the jawbone. Knocked four teeth out too. Son-of-bitch's head swelled up like a melon.'

Charlie laughed. 'That's why they call you Bull. Cos you went at him like a bull.'

'Yeah. That's so.' The sheriff looked pleased.

'You told that one before, Sheriff,' Charlie said. 'Anyhow, this Chinaman's got a reputation. They say when he was working on the Pacific railroad, he could pick up a steel rail and walk fifty yards.'

'That's bullshit. Ain't no Chinaman alive could've got the drop on me when I was younger,' Bull reflected. 'Ain't no one signed up for the fight yet. Ten years ago, I would've been first in the ring and last out.' He turned to Jack. 'How about you, you got the mettle for it?'

'Not me.' Jack grinned. 'I got a full set of teeth an' I aim to keep 'em.'

Bull glanced at him contemptuously. 'Young fellas these days. Seems like nobody ain't got the pep no more. Anyhow, I can't stay here talkin' all afternoon. I got paperwork.' He turned on his heel. 'Seeya Charlie.' Then he said to Jack, 'I got my eye on you, mister.'

After he had left the saloon, Charlie put down the glass he had been polishing and nodded towards the door. 'Don't take no notice of that,' he said. 'That's just ol' Bull talkin'. Anyways, he ain't gone back to do no paperwork. He's slung up a hammock in one of the cells where it's cool. He'll be asleep in five minutes. That's his regular afternoon. One of the deputies told me.

'I tell you what,' Charlie continued. 'Ol' Bull weren't no real boxer, whatever he says. He used to get so mad he'd forget what he was doing and headbutt the other fighters. No-one would fight him in the end, on account of the headbuttin'. 'Course he went around tellin' folks that everyone was afraid to fight him.

'I tell you somethin' else.' He leaned confidentially across the bar. 'When he's liquored up, he ain't careful who he hits, neither. We had a whore in here a year back. Blacklake has 'em brought down from Dodge when he has a mind to, just like he's gonna do this weekend.

'Anyways, one night Bull drank most of a bottle of old sheep-dip and took her upstairs. No-one thought nothin' of it except a while later there was all this screamin' and yellin' and commotion. You could hear Bull's voice damning her to hell an' back and her screamin' to wake the devil. There was some mighty fight going on up there. We let it go for a while, then me and the fella that brought the whores from Dodge hightailed it up them stairs to make sure no one got hurt.

'Well, it was too late for that. The girl was lyin' on the floor with her body all twisted round and Bull was sittin' on the bed with the empty bottle in his hand. I thought her back was broke at first, but she was all right.'

'What did Bull say about it?'

'Nothin'. Just said he'd rather have a bottle of sheep-dip any day. Mind you, he had just drunk a whole bottle all to himself.'

'What happened to the girl?'

'Fella from Dodge took her out to the wagon. In the morning he collected up the other girls and took 'em back to where they come from. Blacklake was mad as hell. He had to go all the way up to Dodge to find a different cathouse next time he wanted girls brung down.'

Charlie looked at Jack. 'You won't go sayin' nothin' about that to no one? That's between you an' me. Bull would be mad as hell if that got out.'

'I bet he can get mad too. I won't say nothin'.'

3

Jack pushed open the door to the livery stable. It was dark inside. Bright lines of sunlight pierced the wooden walls. The horses shifted in their stalls at the entry of someone new. As his eyes adjusted to the darkness, Jack could see that the horses were all neatly brushed and had been fed and watered. There was a hayloft above them. The stable floor had been swept. A yard broom was propped against the ladder.

Jack called out a 'hello there,' but there was no answer. He walked the length of the stables to the door at the back. Outside, there was a fig tree, a patch of young corn and a chicken hutch with a group of chickens pecking in the dust in front of it. A man was asleep on a blanket on the ground in the shade of the fig tree, with his hat covering his face. Jack nudged the man's foot with the toe of his boot. He instantly sprang awake.

'You take care of the stable?' Jack said.

'S'right.' The man was a Comanche Indian. He was tall and strongly built, except for his left arm which was withered and hung uselessly at his side, knotted in the sleeve of his shirt. His hair was tied in long plaits and he wore a torn and faded checked shirt and torn denim pants. He was barefoot. Round his neck there was a carved wooden cross on a leather thong.

'You must be Moses,' Jack said.

'S'right.'

'Well, I've got a horse and a mule here I'd like you to look after. Feed and water 'em. We ain't been so far today, but they've been out in the sun. How much d'you charge?'

'Ten cents overnight feed and water and brush down.' Moses's eyes were fixed on the Indian charm round Jack's neck. It was a necklace, red beads alternating with strips of bleached, white bone threaded together.

'That's cheap,' Jack said.

'Where d'you get that?' Moses indicated the necklace.

'Indian gave it to me.'

'Comanche from up around Missouri,' Moses said. 'She must have liked you.'

'Saved my life.' Jack said. 'I was workin' on a ranch up there one spring, keepin' a lookout for wolves to keep 'em off the calves. I was camped out by the Missouri River an' three guys jumped me. Stole my horse and left me beat up on the riverbank. When I woke up, there was these Indians lookin' after me. They'd found me unconscious and took me back to their village. Treated me with their medicine, gave me food, gave me a place to rest up. I couldn't understand a thing they said, but it didn't seem to matter. One of the squaws gave me this as I was leavin'. I've wore it ever since. I guess it was meant to be a good-luck charm. Ain't had much luck since I was given it though, good nor bad.'

Moses walked back through the barn to bring the animals inside. He settled them in stalls near the door. Jack began to take the pack off the mule. 'Can I leave this here?'

'Sure,' Moses said. 'What you got in it?'

'Tools. Just about everythin',' Jack said. 'I'm lookin' for a place. Somewhere to stay for a while.'

'You come to work on the cattle drive?'

'Nope. I'm through with ridin' for a livin'.'

Moses looked at him hard. 'Never seen a white man with an Indian charm round his neck before.'

'Well, I never seen a Comanche with a cross round his neck neither,' Jack said. Neither man smiled. 'You live here?' Jack asked.

'Mr Blacklake says I can live here on account of there ain't no water at my place. Anyways, he needed someone to look after the horses.'

'That all right by you?'

Moses looked surprised at the question. 'If it's what the Lord wills for me, mister, then I must abide by it. Nobody don't never usually ask me what I think,' he added.

'Miss Adela, I declare that was the finest piece of pie ever handed to a man on the whole panhandle.' Bull dabbed crumbs of pastry from his moustache with a linen serviette in a flourish of good manners.

'Nathan Brown, you're exaggerating again,' Adela said playfully, but she nevertheless enjoyed the compliment.

They were sitting in Adela's parlour at the back of the schoolhouse. Bull felt awkward amidst all the feminine touches in the room: the embroidered tablecloth, the starched napkins, the small china plates and silver knives. His backside was too wide for the upright chairs and his hands were too clumsy for the china.

Adela saw that underneath his great bulk and boorish manners he was desperate to impress her but did not truly know how. He called on her every week. She had been pleased by his attentions at first. But, after a while, she grew tired of his flattery. His compliments on her cooking, on her hair or the flowers on her parlour table began to seem hollow. She realized he was behaving how he thought a man should behave towards a woman. It was this that made his manner so stiff and awkward. If truth be told, she preferred the resentful company of little Zachariah Johnson and the like. There was no awkwardness or false compliments with them.

When, a year ago, Bull had asked Adela to marry him, she suspected he had asked her brother's permission first. Clovis had suddenly started telling her what a good man he was, how loyal he had been in helping to build up the Diamondback and how a woman on the panhandle needed looking after. Adela guessed what was coming.

Sure enough, after more compliments and more flattery, Bull Brown broached the subject. He begun by reminding her that her eyesight was getting worse, so that in the future she would not be able to carry on with her schoolteaching. They had known each other for so long, he had said, and, as she was not getting any younger, they should tie the knot.

Adela was hurt, in a way she had not expected, to think that this was the best he could do for her. She merely told him, taking care not to betray her sadness, that for the foreseeable future the school was her life and she wished for no other. She even suspected that Bull himself was privately relieved she had turned him down. The routine of weekly visits continued.

The sunlight through the parlour window shone on Bull's bald head. 'Well, Nathan,' she said, 'what has been going on in town this week? You know I rely on you for news. Being so taken up, as I am, with teaching the children their letters.'

Bull reflected. 'They're preparing for the drive out at the Diamondback. Theyll have finished cutting out the herd in a coupla days. Clovis has arranged a prizefight in the saloon as a send-off. The men are looking forward to that.'

'Oh Nathan,' Adela said, teasing him. 'You know how I feel about that saloon.'

Bull didn't get the joke. 'I do, Miss Adela,' he affirmed pompously, 'and I shall make it my sworn duty as sheriff to make sure there is no drunkenness or bad behaviour.'

Adela recognized the half-truth at once. Some time ago she had heard a rumour about a girl who had been injured in the saloon. Some people said that Nathan Brown was to blame. She wondered about the injured girl again, but did not dare ask him.

'Another thing,' Bull added. 'There's a drifter in town. Jus' rode in this afternoon. Looks like the usual kinda saddle tramp. Wouldn't trust him as far as I could spit.' Adela grimaced at the distasteful remark. 'He'll be lookin' round for a place to stay. If he comes knockin', you turn him away. I already told him drifters don't stay long in this town.'

'Well, have you spoken to this man, Nathan?'

'Told him to move on out,' Brown said with a smirk.

Adela suddenly loathed this brute of a man who paid her these empty compliments, sitting there in her sunlit parlour with his fat legs planted apart so he didn't topple off her best dining chair. How dare he tell her not to rent her room? And how typical it was of him not to have given the man a chance to explain himself. Again, she omitted to tell him that she had already met Jack and that she had already promised him the room.

In the years after the war, Adela had seen many men passing through the town, though there were fewer of them now. They were ghosts, haunted by the death and destruction they had witnessed. Often, their families had been killed and their homes destroyed. They would rent her room and if they did not have any money, she would let them sleep there anyway. They would only stay a night or two before moving on, in search of whatever it was they were looking for. Her heart used to bleed for them when they sat in this very parlour telling her their stories. How dare this arrogant, opinionated sheriff tell her not to open her door to men like that.

'Well now, Mr Brown, I think it's time you were getting along.' Adela smiled sweetly at him. 'I know you're a very busy man, being sheriff.'

'Well, yes I suppose I am.' He took the hint and stood up to leave. 'I'll be ridin' out to the Diamondback now to talk to your brother about the arrangements for Saturday. Make sure everythin' goes off proper.' He hesitated, 'I don't suppose you'd like to accompany me, Miss Adela? We could take the buggy. It's a fine, warm evening for a ride.'

Adela laughed. She took care not to mention that Clem was resting in her spare bedroom and she intended to watch over him that evening. 'You're too kind, Nathan. But if you men are discussing business, you won't want me around. I'll just stay here and tend to my chores.'

Jack sat on a hay bale and watched Moses brush the bay. 'You can leave him to me, mister,' said the Comanche. 'You don' have to wait.'

'Got to find myself somewhere to stay,' Jack said. 'I can maybe have a room at the back of the schoolhouse tomorrow.'

'Miss Adela's place.' Moses smiled. 'That's Goldie, her horse, right there.' He indicated a beautiful, young chestnut mare. 'Her brother picked it out for her.'

'Fine lookin' horse,' Jack said.

'She's a kind lady, Miss Adela,' Moses said. 'She's been nice to me since I was a kid. I look after Goldie real good for her.'

Moses carried on brushing with firm, regular strokes. 'You can bed down in the hay loft, if you've a mind to. Don't make no difference to me.'

'Thanks,' Jack said. 'I been sleeping on the ground so long, that sounds like a mighty nice offer. You live here all the time?'

'Since the creek water dried up at the mission.' Moses passed on this information with no emotion. He didn't look at Jack and concentrated on his work.

'I came into town through there,' said Jack. 'I was camped on the ridge last night, a mile or two outa town. Musta been a nice place once.'

34

Moses stopped brushing and patted the horse's flank. 'It was where I was brung up,' he said. 'There was a garden. We used to keep a sow out back. I lived there since I was a kid. Since they took me in.'

Jack waited for him to continue. 'My people gave me to Pastor Joe's wife, Mary, to look after when I was a baby. Maybe on accounta my arm. Maybe they didn't think I was goin' to live. They gave me to her in a basket. That's how come they called me Moses. They raised me like I was their own. They was tryin' to start a mission to take the Lord to the Comanche and bring the Comanche to the Lord. That's what they used to say.'

'Musta bin good people,' Jack said.

'The influenza took 'em, three winters ago. Carried 'em off to Paradise.'

'So how come you moved in here?'

'No water from the creek. Mr Blacklake said I could come here. The Comanche people won't take me in now. Didn't have much choice.'

Moses turned to Jack and looked him directly in the eye. 'I own that land. There's legal papers says so. The Pastor Joe left it to me in his will. He told me before he went to be with Jesus. He showed me the paper. He read it out to me, just like he used to read out stories outa the Bible. The man from the bank came out and signed the will paper as a witness. He took the paper to the bank, jus' like Pastor Joe told him to, for safe keepin', he says.'

'What made the creek dry up?' Jack asked.

'Just did. One day, it just dried up.'

'There's water out there. I seen the cottonwoods. Two, three stands of them.'

Moses smiled grimly. 'I know. But who's gonna help me dig a well?'

'Mighty nice offer of lettin' me bed down in the hayloft,' Jack said.

Despite his impassive face, Jack could tell that Moses was pleased he was going to sleep at the stable. Moses brewed up some coffee for him on a small fire in the yard and gave him some hard-tack biscuits. Every time he looked at Jack, his eyes fell on the Comanche charm around his neck.

As dusk fell, Jack settled into the hay to sleep. If he couldn't have a bed, then this surely was the next best thing. Moses was sleeping out back somewhere and the horses were quiet and still. Daylight faded and soon the stable was in darkness. The scratching and scampering of a few rats was the only sound, but this was not enough to keep Jack awake. He soon slipped into his first unbroken sleep for weeks.

4

Jack woke at first light to the sound of Moses feeding the horses below him. He lay back in the straw. In his long journey south across country through the Kansas territories, he had seen town after town battling to survive against the land, the climate, the Indians. He had met hard, determined people everywhere. That's the way you had to be in the West. Some of them were good, some of them were bad, he reflected. Most of them were both. He had decided what to do. This town was not much different from any other. It was a place he could stay.

Later, as the coffee pot bubbled on the fire in the yard, Jack offered to help Moses dig a well on the old mission, to make the place habitable again. 'In return for a half-share in the place.'

'You want a half-share with me?' Moses asked, incredulous. 'You wanna live there with me?'

'We'd dig the well first, then we'd repair the house. We'd sow some corn, plant potatoes. We'd have chickens. Even grow our own tobacco if we wanted. You could carry on working here to keep some money comin' in, while I did most of the repairin'.'

'My, my,' Moses said. 'Never thought I'd live at the old mission again. Praise be.'

'Only thing is,' Jack said, 'you got to be able to prove it's yours. You got to have the deeds. I heard the Diamondback drive their cattle through there now.'

'When Pastor Joe was alive, Mr Blacklake wanted to buy the mission off him and close it down so he could run his cattle through,' Moses told Jack. 'Pastor Joe wouldn't sell on account of how he was doin' the Lord's work there, tryin' to reach out to the Comanche people. Blacklake wanted him to come into town. He said he'd build a church for him. Pastor Joe said if Blacklake wanted a church in town, he'd build it anyways, he just wanted him off the land.'

'The town ain't got no church,' Jack said.

'Miss Adela used to come out to the mission to visit Mary, the pastor's wife. They was real good friends. They used to cook the food together and read the Bible stories to me. Miss Adela tried to teach me to read. The townsfolk wouldn't let me go to Miss Adela's school in town on account of me bein' a Comanche, so when Miss Adela came out to the mission she used to give me lessons. I can read some, but I ain't much good at it. She was kind to me right from when I was a child. That's why I take real special good care of her horse, Goldie, now.'

'So,' Jack said, 'when the pastor and his wife died, Miss Adela didn't visit the mission no more? And that's when the creek dried up and Blacklake started running his cattle through?'

'I ain't sayin' nothin',' Moses said. 'Mr Blacklake lets

me stay here cus I ain't got nowhere else to stay. He lets me work here an' that's how I live. If the creek dries up that must be the Lord workin'.'

Jack leaned back against the fig tree. 'Well,' he said. 'That don't change nothin'. You still got to be able to prove the place is yours.'

'The pastor put the deeds in a black box in the bank,' Moses said.

An hour later, Jack stood in front of an iron grille in the town bank. On the other side of the grille was Clarence Fayette. This shy young man had jumped at the chance of being promoted to manager when he was working in a sizeable branch of the bank in Kansas and living at home with his mother. But he had since found that living in this isolated Texas cattle town and dealing with its people rattled his nerves. He seemed unable to give Jack a straight answer to his request to see the deeds of the old mission.

Everything concerning land claims had to be dealt with through the bank's agent, he said, and the agent was required to be a qualified lawyer because of the obvious legal implications of the claims. When Jack asked where the agent was, Clarence became even less clear and started to say that in not all circumstances was it possible for there to be an agent as such. Because of the fast expansion of banking in the West and the number of cattle towns springing up on the Western plains, there was also not always a lawyer available either. Jack bit his tongue.

'Where are the deeds and how can I see them?' Jack asked firmly, trying not to raise his voice. Clarence was beginning to squirm. He had been instructed to hand over all documents concerning land and land claims to the major landowner in the area. This was Clovis Blacklake, owner of the Diamondback Ranch. 'Who instructed you?' Jack persisted. Clarence appeared to be in need of a drink of water. His mouth had gone dry and it was difficult for him to articulate. His hands shook. 'He did,' he said.

'Clovis Blacklake ordered you to hand over all the deeds and land claims to him?' Jack said, incredulous.

'In the absence of other suitable persons, it is in the discretion of the local branch to appoint an agent to oversee land documents,' squeaked Clarence, quoting from the bank's manual.

'Well, I'll be jiggered. You're telling me you handed over the deeds to the mission and all the other land on this part of the panhandle to Clovis Blacklake?'

Clarence nodded vigorously, beads of sweat standing out on his forehead. 'Mr Blacklake owns this part of the panhandle.'

'Not all of it,' snarled Jack. He leaned forward until the rim of his hat was touching the grille and spoke slowly and deliberately. 'The next time I come in here, I want the deeds to the mission property and the pastor's will which was deposited here, ready for me to collect so they can be returned to the rightful owner. Are you understanding me, mister?'

Clarence backed away from the iron grille as if he was afraid Jack might suddenly burst through it. 'Y-yes,' he said trembling.

Deeds or no deeds, Jack called in at Johnson's Hardware on his way back to the stables. He bought shovels, a pickaxe and a handpick as well as buckets and rope. Mrs. Johnson herself served him. She was a cheerful, garrulous woman of about fifty.

'Plannin' on doin' some diggin?' she said.

'Yeah,' Jack said. 'The old mission ain't got a well and the creek's all dried up.'

Mrs Johnson was surprised. 'Nobody ain't lived there for years, since the influenza carried the pastor and his wife off, poor dears. That land belongs to Mr Blacklake, don't it? Most everythin' else round here does. He plannin' on buildin' out there? Wouldn't surprise me. This whole town wouldn't be here if it wasn't for him buildin' it.'

'Don't suppose it would,' Jack said pleasantly.

Back at the stables Jack noticed that Moses had put his shotgun out, ready to take with them. Beside it was a Comanche tomahawk with feathers decorating the handle. 'Won't get much diggin' done with this,' Jack said.

Moses frowned. 'Found it stuck in the stable door this morning. Happens every now and then. Some young brave dares to ride into town, throw his tomahawk and then ride out again. It's a threat to me for livin' with the white man. These young braves weren't even born when I was living out at the Mission. They're just hotheads showin' off to each other. I'll take the scattergun along for company.'

'I never heard no one in the night,' Jack said.

'You'll never hear 'em. They're quiet as a snake on its belly. You just gotta keep your eyes peeled.'

'I'll do that,' Jack said.

The mission house had been built in the shadow of a sheer red sandstone escarpment which stretched for miles in either direction. The house was situated beside the entrance to a narrow canyon which contained a dry riverbed and led, after a few miles, up on to the bluff. Some quarrying had been done there and a large section of the entrance to the gully had been hacked untidily away. There were several stands of cottonwood trees along the foot of the cliff and at the mouth of the gully. Their silver leaves shimmered in the dry plains breeze. Beside the cottonwoods were clumps of hackberry bushes, but nothing else grew there any more. The ground was hard and dry.

The walls and floor of the mission house were still standing and most of the roof was intact. It was a simple structure made of cheap cottonwood. Many of the planks out of which the walls had been made were warped and needed replacing. The veranda was partly collapsed, as someone had slung a lasso round one of the supporting posts and tried to pull it away. Moses untied the picks, shovels and rope from the back of the mule.

The two men headed for the densest thicket of cotton woods which was growing between the house and the gully. This was the place for the well. Jack drove a stake into the ground, looped a rope over it and, holding the rope taut, walked round the stake, marking a circle in the dust. 'That's the easy part.' He grinned.

'I'll start it,' Moses said. He knelt on all fours and broke up the surface of the ground with the handpick, working his way round inside the circle. Jack followed behind him shovelling aside the dry, broken earth. They found an easy rhythm, hacking and digging, and worked on for almost an hour.

The sun was climbing in the sky. They had dug down to knee height. They put down their tools and took a break, leaning against the trunk of a cottonwood, sipping water from their canteens. Neither man spoke. After a while, Jack stood up and took hold of a pickaxe. Moses grabbed a short-handled shovel. They carried on as before, but this time Jack went ahead, breaking up the ground, and Moses followed. They quickly settled into their rhythm and carried on for another hour.

At midday they stopped work to eat the beef jerky that Moses had packed for them and to take more sips of water from their canteens. They moved the horses and the mule round behind the mission house into a patch of shade. The heat and the work sapped their energy. Jack was surprised and impressed at how Moses was able to keep up with him with just his one good arm. Moses, for his part, was still amazed that Jack wanted him for a partner, when, although the townspeople were not unkind to him, usually he was ignored.

The men carried on working like this. They took turns with the tasks and stopped for a drink every hour. They worked against the heat from the sun and pushed into the ache in their shoulders, encouraged by seeing the well grow deeper with every shovelful of dirt. Neither man wanted to be the first to break the rhythm. The earth was baked hard and it was stony. So far, there was no sign of water. By mid-afternoon, the hole was at waist height. The deeper they got, Moses worked with the handpick and Jack shovelled, as Moses couldn't raise the spade high enough to sling the earth out of the well.

When, at last, they had had enough, Jack scrambled out

43

of the hole and leaned back to haul Moses up after him.

'We got company,' Jack whispered in his ear as he pulled him up. 'Behind me, on the ridge.'

Moses looked up over Jack's shoulder. A Comanche brave was sitting on a palomino pony watching them. The horse and the rider were as still as if they had been carved out of stone. 'He's been there most of the morning,' Moses said. 'He's just letting us know that he's seen us.' Jack turned and looked up at the brave, who immediately wheeled his horse around and disappeared over the other side of the bluff.

'It ain't nothin',' Moses said. 'He's just watchin' what goes on.'

'I thought those braves weren't too keen on you?'

'They ain't. But he won't do nothin'. We ain't harmin' no one.'

Jack couldn't help noticing that Moses kept the scattergun cradled across his lap on the ride back to town.

Clem had been pronounced fit enough to ride out to the Diamondback, so the room behind the schoolhouse was free. It was furnished with a closet, cotton curtains, a small table with a china water jug and a bowl on it, a straight-backed chair and, to Jack's delight, a single iron-framed bed with a thin horsehair mattress. He couldn't remember when he had last slept in a bed with springs. He lay down on it immediately to test it out, his boots sticking over the end. Adela said she was preparing supper and he should get washed up.

Adela was glad of the company. She had cooked braised rabbit and spring greens for Jack but ate nothing herself.

44

The way Jack had taken charge of the injured Clem and carried him straight to the schoolhouse had impressed her. It showed a decisiveness in his nature which the local men seemed to lack, despite their cowboy swagger. She was also mindful that she wanted to talk to him to spite Bull Brown, even if the sheriff wasn't there to see it. She sat at the other end of the parlour table ready for conversation.

'I hope you'll be comfortable out back,' Adela said pleasantly.

'It's a fine room, ma'am,' Jack said. 'Last night I was in a hayloft and the night before I was on the ground. It'll be luxury to me.'

'I shall take the buggy out to the Diamondback and stay there while you're here. My brother insists on it whenever there's someone stayin'. But I'll be back in the mornin'. I guess you'll be wantin' some breakfast.'

'Thank you, ma'am, but I'll be leavin' at first light. I'm helpin' Moses dig a well out at the old mission. We aim to make a good start before the day heats up.'

Jack saw a shadow pass across her face and watched her cheerfulness recede. 'But no one lives out at the mission now. My brother lets Moses work at the stables. The minister and his wife died three years ago.'

'Ma'am,' Jack said firmly, 'the minister left the place to Moses, all signed and legal in his will. Mr Fayette at the bank was his witness.' He looked directly into Adela's eyes as he spoke.

'I don't know anything about that,' she said. 'I nursed Mary when she was sick with the influenza.' She turned her head away. 'My brother is a good man, Mr Just. He lets

45

Moses live at the stables.'

'I know he does, ma'am.'

Adela took Jack's plate as soon as he had finished. Her keenness to talk to him had suddenly transformed into a nervousness concerning what he might tell her. Jack sensed this.

'Mighty nice horse you got down at the stables,' he said. 'Moses pointed her out to me. You had her long?'

Adela smiled. 'She's a beauty. Clovis gave her to me for my birthday two years back. She was born out on the Diamondback. One of the cowboys broke her for me.'

'She sure is fine-lookin',' Jack said, 'one of the finest I've seen.'

'Mr Just,' Adela said suddenly. 'When you've finished digging the well out at the old mission, what will you do then?'

'Guess I'll help Moses repairin' the house,' Jack said. 'Intend to stay awhile. I've bin travellin' a long time, ma'am. That could be a nice place out there, if there was water.'

'It used to be,' Adela said. 'Mary had a lovely garden. They kept a cow out there and a pig out back. But in front of the house there were flowers. Carpets of bluebonnets at just this time of year, if there had been a wet spring. Marigolds like flame and wild azaleas. . . .' She caught herself. 'I'm sorry,' she said. 'I was remembering.'

'I'd like to have seen it,' Jack smiled.

'I best be getting out to the Diamondback,' Adela said quickly.

'Let me walk down to the stable and fetch your horse for you.'

Adela caught his eye. 'That's mighty kind of you, Mr Just, but I'm not so old and infirm yet that I can't fetch my own horse.'

'I didn't mean. . . .'

Adela laughed. 'It was a mighty nice offer. I mean it.'

'Call me Jack,' Jack said.

'And you can call me Adela.'

On her ride out to the Diamondback, Adela considered the gentle-mannered stranger she had recently met: how he had calmly taken charge of the injured Clem; how he had spoken without anger or bitterness about the terrible war, which was rare even now in the South; how he had offered to fetch her horse from the stable. In his newly rented room, Jack considered the kindly, myopic schoolteacher: how efficiently she had tended Clem's injuries and provided him with a new shirt; how she had seemed genuinely interested in his story; how, in her eyes, her brother could do no wrong.

5

Jack collected Moses from the stables at first light. Another tomahawk was buried deep in the stable door. Inside, Moses appeared unconcerned. He had packed their saddlebags with enough food and canteens of water to see them through the day. But again, he took his shotgun with him.

Jack wrenched the tomahawk out of the stable door and presented it to Moses. 'He musta came on foot,' he said. 'Didn't hear no horse.'

'Those braves can move quiet,' Moses said. 'I seed 'em hunt.'

Out at the mission, Jack half-expected the picks, shovels and other equipment to have been interfered with. But they were in the same neat pile at the back of the old house where he and Moses had left them. Moses made a fire and put a pot of coffee on to brew. Jack inspected their work of the previous day. The sides of the hole held good. Five feet down, the earth floor was cold and bone-dry. Jack had the feeling that they were about to hit solid rock. He jumped down into the hole and began breaking up the

48

floor with his pick.

The men dug and shovelled as they had the previous day. The ground was getting harder the deeper they went. After an hour they had got down another two feet. It was becoming impractical to shovel the broken earth and stone out of the well. Without Jack asking him, Moses went off and felled a young cottonwood, cleaned off all the side branches from the trunk with a hand-axe and dragged it over to the well. The two of them manoeuvred it across the centre where they had dug, Moses from the outside and Jack from down in the hole.

Moses tied an iron bucket on to the end of a rope and lowered it over the tree trunk for Jack to fill with earth. He hauled bucket after bucket, emptied them carefully and lowered them back down. After another hour, they changed places.

Standing on the lip of the well, Jack scanned the line of hills. There was no brave there like the previous day but he still had the feeling they were being watched. The scattergun never left Moses's side. He even took it down into the well with him when it was his turn to do the digging. The heat, which had been building throughout the morning, now beat off the sides of the cliff and shimmered like twisted glass over the plain. Jack called down to Moses to take a break.

They sat in the shade of the cottonwoods, sipping from their canteens. They could measure the hours of work by the ache across their shoulders. It felt good though, as they could see in front of them the hole and the mound of earth they had created. 'Gettin' close,' Jack said. 'Must be. These old cottonwood roots don't go much deeper

49

and that's where the water'll be.' Moses seemed not to hear him and was watching the entrance to the dry creek, behind the house. He picked up the scattergun which lay beside him and held it across his lap.

A few moments later three riders emerged from the mouth of the creek. They walked their horses slowly over the stones in the dry riverbed. Jack recognized Bull Brown as one of the riders. The other two were taller and deputy's stars glinted on their shirts. All three wore six-guns and had Winchesters tied to their saddles. They rode slowly, straight up to Jack and Moses, coming to a halt between them and the well.

'Seems like we got ourselves a problem,' Bull sneered, staring hard at Jack.

'No problem here, Sheriff,' Jack said lightly.

'Why don' you get your Injun to put his shotgun down. Combination of guns and Injuns makes me nervous.'

'He can hold on to it if he wants to.' Jack stared straight back at Bull.

Bull leaned forward in his saddle and ignored Jack's last remark. 'The problem we got is that you're trespassin'.' He spoke slowly as if he was explaining something to a fool. 'This land is part of the Diamondback ranch as belongs to Mr Clovis Blacklake. The land to the north of the cliff is Diamondback and the plains to the south is Diamondback. And this here land in the middle is Diamondback too.'

'I bin expectin' you, Sheriff,' Jack said calmly. 'I bin expectin' some kinda misunderstandin' to arise. Because this here land belongs to Moses. It was left to him by the pastor in his will an' it don't belong to nobody else.'

Bull was silent for a moment, then he let out a peal of loud false laughter. 'What d'you think this is? Some kinda reservation?' He looked to the deputies for support. They sniggered obligingly. 'This is cattle country, mister. We cleared the Injuns off this part of the panhandle years ago, before the war. There's a few drifts back every now and then, that's all. As fer ol' Moses here,' he laughed, 'old Moses one arm, Mr Blacklake's good enough to let him clean out the stables so long as he behaves himself. Ain't that so, Moses?'

Moses stared straight ahead of him.

'Old Moses has gone all shy,' Bull said.

'I'm thinkin' that we have work to do,' Jack said coldly. 'We can't hang around here talkin'. You gentlemen will have to leave. The deeds to this property are being taken care of in the bank. I shall be collecting them when I'm back in town. This mission belongs to Moses by law.'

'I am the law here!' roared Bull. 'You don' know nothin'. This here's the panhandle, mister. This land is vacant. It has been annexed to the Diamondback. I'm tellin' you that if this well isn't filled in next time we come by, you'll be coolin' your heels in my jail.' He jerked the reins in his hand. 'Come on, boys.'

They started south across the plain, the quickest route to town.

'There's a cattle drive comin' through here next week, anyhow,' Bull called over his shoulder. 'Ten thousand head. Don' expect there'll be much left of the old mission house after that, anyways.'

Moses and Jack watched them go. Moses nudged Jack's arm and gestured towards the creek. Above them, on the

51

edge of the bluff, a Comanche brave sat on his pony watching them as he had done the previous day. As soon as Jack looked up and saw him, he wheeled his horse around and was gone.

Jack took the short-handled shovel and pick and lowered himself down into the well, taking care not to damage the sides. As soon as his boots hit the floor, he felt it. The well bottom was two inches deep in wet mud. Water was seeping up through the floor and in through the side nearest the stand of cottonwoods. He shouted to Moses and set about slapping mud into the bucket. The men worked faster, spurred on by their success, seeming to relish the burning ache across their backs and shoulders. For the moment, they pushed thoughts of Bull Brown and his threats out of their minds.

Mud was easier to dig than the baked earth, so they made good progress. Another three feet down, Jack shored up the sides of the well. He drove in planks which Moses salvaged from the porch of the old mission, down into the mud and nailed on crosspieces to keep them in place. The cottonwood would rot quickly, but would hold until they could substitute hardwood or some iron stakes if they could get them. The seepage of water had become a steady trickle and was beginning to collect in pools on the well bottom.

'There'll be enough to use by morning,' Jack said.

Moses smiled grimly. 'Maybe,' he said.

Clovis Blacklake sat at his desk in a sumptuous office at the Diamondback ranch. This was the heart of his empire. An enormous pair of longhorns was mounted on the wall above his polished oak desk. Shelves of account books and ledgers lined the wall behind it. Open French windows gave a view over the ranchland. Miles of unbroken country, once populated by buffalo and bands of Comanche, now a vast, empty space, was home to his herd of near 20,000 head.

With typical thoroughness, Blacklake had been re-reading the land claim and the deeds to the mission. It reminded him of the early days. The pastor had arrived on the panhandle at the same time as Blacklake started buying up parcels of land which would later be put together to make up the Diamondback Ranch. The pastor had claimed the acreage at the mouth of Bluebonnet Canyon and built himself and his wife a homestead there. If the land claim's agent had been quicker off the mark, Blacklake would have been able to register a claim there before the pastor. Blacklake knew he should have dealt with it at the time, but Adela had immediately become friends with the pastor's wife. Back then, Clovis had wished to encourage this friendship as he worried about his sister. There was little enough suitable female company for her on the panhandle, so he had let the matter go.

Eventually, Blacklake had offered to buy the acreage from the pastor when he realized the creek would provide a short cut for his cattle drives north. But Blacklake found him to be a stubborn, deluded man who seemed to be set on converting the whole Comanche nation to Christianity single handed. He didn't realize that the Indians found him ridiculous and laughed at him behind his back. They gave him a crippled child to raise, who would have been a burden to the tribe. It had been intended as an insult. The boy turned out to be the only convert he ever made.

Once again, in deference to his sister Adela's feelings, Blacklake had not taken over the mission when the minister and his wife passed. Instead, he had the stream dammed up on the plains near its source. The Indian, whom the minister had willed the place to, couldn't live there without water, so he had let him mind the stables for whatever tips he could make. Again, he knew that good-natured Adela, whose esteem he held dear, would take this to be an act of generosity.

Now, he had heard from Adela that a drifter had come into town and was intending to move out to the old mission together with the Indian. It was ridiculous how he had to spend time pussyfooting round these people, he thought. He leaned back in his chair and drew heavily on his cigar. The notion of building a homestead in the middle of the best cattle country on the panhandle was absurd. That it should block the route of what promised to be the most financially rewarding cattle drive he had ever made could not be allowed. He was waiting to hear what the drifter's reaction had been to Bull Brown's visit.

Another thing that was playing on his mind was what an irritation Bull Brown had become. Bull and he went way back. He had not forgotten that his early success in the cattle business would not have been possible without Bull's help. Bull was as hard a man as he himself was, Clovis had often thought, only ten times more stupid.

Recently though, Bull had decided he wanted to hitch up with Adela. Although the idea of having Bull as a brother-in-law was far from appealing on one level, Clovis knew that he would always be the boss. His poor, half-blind sister needed looking after and Clovis could ensure that Bull would provide for her. The only problem with Bull, from Clovis's point of view, was his temper. Clovis suspected Bull was at the back of the incident where one of his best hands had been jumped on outside the saloon, though he doubted he would ever completely get to the bottom of it.

Blacklake's thoughts went back to the mission. Just as he was preparing for his best and biggest cattle drive, this drifter had turned up out of nowhere, got himself living at the back of Adela's schoolroom and was trying to claim the mission property. He was going to have to make use of Bull Brown and his temper, Blacklake thought. It would be easiest all round if the deeds became misplaced, too. An Indian and a drifter: he smiled to himself. Hardly worth worrying about at all. He lit a match and held up the deed by a corner. The flame licked through the parchment in seconds. He did the same to the minister's will and the original land claim. He brushed the flakes of ash off his desk on to the floor.

Back in town, Jack handed his horse over to Moses outside the schoolhouse. Adela had promised him a meal after his hard day well-digging. Moses would take care of himself as usual down at the stable. Fortunately, his scattergun had come in handy and he had brought home two young rabbits tied to his saddle.

Jack knew he would have to tread carefully with Adela. He liked her and it was obvious that she liked him. But he had a feeling that he was going to be meeting Clovis, her brother, soon. Jack knew that he was going to have to stand up to him over rights to the mission property. This put him in a thoughtful mood. He had never heard of a cattleman yet who would willingly compromise over land, particularly if the land meant a shorter route for a cattle drive. Jack let himself into the schoolhouse.

The schoolroom was empty. The children's slates were neatly piled on a front row desk. The blackboard had been wiped clean and a broom was propped up in the corner. The soft sunlight of late afternoon filled the room and in it Jack noticed a vase lying broken in a pool of water beside the teacher's desk. Violets were scattered around it on the floor. Jack called out to Adela, but there was no answer. There was no one in the parlour or the kitchen on the other side of the schoolroom. Jack called out again. Still nothing. Jack went back to the schoolroom and collected the pieces of broken vase and the dying flowers and, unsure what to do with domestic things like this, carried them through to the kitchen and left them on the scrubbed wooden table.

Jack was surprised to find himself disappointed that Adela was not there. He went to his room out back, poured water from the china jug into the bowl and began to wash his hands and face. The cool water was balm to his parched skin. He rubbed water through his hair and round his neck, letting the heat of the afternoon soak away.

Not sure of what to do, Jack picked up a heavy package hidden away under the bed. It was wrapped in a thin piece of deer hide and tied with a strip of leather. It was his gunbelt and two Peacemakers. He took the guns out of their holsters and lay them carefully beside the belt. He inspected them carefully, one after the other. He flipped open the gate and peered into the empty chambers, held the barrel up to the light and cocked and recocked the hammer of each pistol to check the firing mechanism. The guns were clean and well-oiled. Jack took twelve cartridges out of the belt and loaded the chamber of each gun. When he was finished, he replaced them in their holsters and hung the gunbelt on the hook on the back of the door.

There was still no sign of Adela. Maybe one of the schoolchildren had fallen sick and Adela had gone to check on him, Jack thought. He lay back on the bed to rest. His muscles ached after the day's digging. The bed was still a luxury, so he might as well enjoy it while he could.

He woke sometime later and was surprised to find it was growing dark. He sensed immediately that the schoolhouse building was still empty. Adela had not returned. He swung his legs over the side of the bed and sat up. He was ravenous. He decided to see if he could get some food at the saloon.

There were a few cowhands playing an early evening hand of poker at one of the tables and two more at the bar, staring into their beer. Jack noticed that Clem was not there. In fact, he had not seen him since he had taken him to Adela's. The place was decorated with long loops of red paper streamers round the walls and across the front of a stage which had been erected at the far end of the saloon. Posters advertising the prize fight were tacked at regular intervals down the walls. On the bar, a board was propped up against a wooden crate. On it were chalked the words '$100 Purse. Lick the Chinaman. Sign up here.' The writing was an uneven patchwork of capital letters. No one had signed up.

'Ain't got no food left,' Charlie said to Jack's request. 'Diamondback boys were in earlier and licked the skillet clean. Anyhow, I thought you were down at Lemonade Lil's. She forgotten how to cook?'

'Nope,' Jack said. 'She ain't there.'

'She'll be out at the Diamondback,' Charlie said. 'Schoolhouse or the Diamondback, the only two places she ever is. Or Mrs. Johnson's.'

'Thanks.'

Charlie leaned towards him across the bar. Jack knew there was a piece of gossip coming. 'Everyone's got wind of you and old Moses diggin' that well at the mission,' he said confidentially. 'You might want to take a walk down to the stables. Them two deputies and a coupla roughneck cowhands was talking about paying a call on the Indian a while ago. Bought a bottle of old sheep-dip.'

'When was this?' Jack said, but he was already leaving.

'Half an hour back,' Charlie called after him, 'maybe more.'

As he ran the last few yards towards the stable, Jack could hear what was going on. The whining, taunting voices of the deputies, the sounds of struggle, Moses groaning in pain. Jack burst through the stable door like a storm. Two cowhands were holding Moses in a kneeling position with his good arm twisted up behind his back. The younger of the deputies, Bill, was holding Moses's head back by his hair with one hand and trying to pour whiskey into his mouth from the bottle in his other hand. The older deputy, Silas, was sitting on a nearby haybale, enjoying the show.

'Come on now, Moses,' Bill yanked his victim's head back again, 'ain't you gonna have a little drink with us?' Whiskey splashed down on Moses's face as he twisted right and left, trying to keep his mouth closed.

'Kick him in the belly again. Cut off his wind. That'll make 'im open his flapper,' Silas said, laughing.

From the doorway Jack launched himself at Bill, knocking the bottle out of his hand and bringing him crashing to the floor. In the same motion he brought back his fist and slammed it into the deputy's jaw. Bill let out a howl of shock, terror and pain at the unexpected attack. The two cowhands released their hold on Moses who immediately collapsed on to the ground.

The cowhands made a grab for Jack, but his right arm was already drawn back for a sock at the nearest man's jaw. He hit him on the side of the face and the cheekbone crunched against his fist. There was a cracking sound as several of the cowhand's teeth broke. The cowhand reeled back, spitting out blood and teeth, moaning with hurt.

The other cowhand changed tack and dived for Jack's legs, bringing him down on top of Bill. The deputy grunted as the breath was knocked out of his body. The moment Jack was down, Silas, who had sprung up from his haybale, aimed a kick at his guts. Jack was winded for a second. Then, from out of nowhere, Moses gave a great roar and hurled himself at Silas, grabbing him in a headlock, just as he aimed another full-force kick at Jack.

No one noticed another man step out of the shadows of

one of the stalls, but everyone heard the distinct click of a
Remington being cocked. The man grabbed Moses by the
hair and shoved the barrel of the handgun against his
temple. Bull Brown had been watching the proceedings
from the start. Moses released his hold on Silas and
everyone froze. Bull's face was purple with rage.

'Let 'im have it, Bull,' Silas yelled. 'Shoot his goddam
brains out.'

Bull glared at Silas, drew his arm back and cracked the
pistol against the side of Moses's skull. Moses reeled as
lightning exploded in his brain. Bull shoved him to one
side and Moses fell across a haybale. Bull pointed the
Remington straight at Jack's head.

'Geddup,' he snarled.

As soon as Jack staggered to his feet Silas and one of the
cowhands each grabbed hold of one of his arms, forcing
them up into a vicious double armlock behind him. Jack
grunted in pain.

'I oughta kill you right here.' Bull pointed the pistol
directly at Jack's face. 'That's an officer of the law you
attacked. I oughta smear your brains all over the walls. I
oughta turn you into cattlefeed. Ain't no one gonna miss
a lousy drifter.'

Silas and the cowhand wrenched their armlocks tighter,
almost breaking Jack's arms at the elbows. Jack grimaced.
Bull clicked the hammer of the Remington shut so that
the gun was no longer cocked. He drew back his arm and
smashed the pistol into the side of Jack's face while the
men held him tight. Then again. Then again. At the third,
slamming blow, Jack's head lolled forward and his body
slumped. The men released his arms and he fell face first,

unconscious on to the ground.

Bull kicked Moses in the ribs. 'You hear me, Injun? You got some cleanin' up to do. You work for Mr Blacklake. He give you this job. Don' you go hanging round with no drifters or gettin' ideas about diggin' no lousy wells.'

Bull turned to the others. 'You four ain't so smart neither. Four o' you, an' you can't take down a drifter and an Injun? I have to do all your work for you? Damn young fools.' He turned to Silas and indicated Jack, who still lay face down on the floor without moving. 'You'n Bill get him on his feet and walk 'im down to the jailhouse and lock him in. Think you can manage that? You cowpunchers best give them a hand jus' in case he wakes up enough to start kickin' off. Then you get yourselves back to the Diamondback. You've had your fun for this evenin'.'

6

'This is absolutely ridiculous. You're treating me like a child.' Adela was hopping mad. She rarely raised her voice against anyone, let alone her own brother. But at the moment, Clovis's treatment of her seemed unfair and unreasonable. 'You're treating me like a prisoner! You know I have to run the school in the mornings. The children rely on me.'

Clovis laughed. 'No child will mind having a few days off school, my dear Adela.'

'I simply do not understand why you are doing this. You've never done anything like it before.' Adela stamped up and down her brother's study. She held her long skirt off the floor to allow herself a brisk pace. Her brother sat back in his leather chair, much amused by her stamping feet and rustling petticoats and waited for her to calm down.

'My dear Adela, I have already explained to you,' Clovis said with forced patience. 'I want you to stay here at the Diamondback with me until after the cattle drive leaves on Monday. The town will be full of terrible people until then. This prizefight has created so much interest, the place will be crowded out. People are coming from all over the panhandle. They'll be setting up tents. They'll be gambling. And there'll be drinking. I have to be there to be in charge, but I do not want my sister to have anything to do with any of this. The panhandle is a man's country, Adela. You know that perfectly well.'

'I have survived in the panhandle for sixteen years, Clovis. I absolutely will not be locked away just because there is a boxing match at the saloon! And what about the children? They'll be arriving at an empty school this morning.'

'I've already taken care of that,' Clovis said sharply. His patience was running out. 'I have asked one of the men to ride into town later this morning and nail a notice to the schoolroom door saying that there will be no school until next Tuesday.'

'What?' Adela was beside herself. 'How dare you do that? I shall tear that notice down as soon as I see it. You have no right to interfere with the running of the school.'

'Enough, Adela,' commanded Clovis. 'My mind is made up. It is absolutely out of the question for you to be in town for the next few days, especially with your condition.'

'Oh!' Adela flounced. 'I was waiting for that. My condition, as you call it, does not stop me running a school. My condition does not stop me living my life. Just because my poor old eyes are not working as well as they should, it does not mean I cannot stay in town.'

'I said enough!' bellowed Clovis. 'I have made up my mind. In a few days, you can go back to town. The school will reopen, you can carry on entertaining Brown when he comes to call on you and that drifter will be long gone. You are too trusting, Adela. That man made an unprovoked attack on one of the deputies last night. Bull Brown has him locked up in the jailhouse. The man you had let the room to.' Clovis smiled condescendingly. 'You may be able to teach children their letters, but you really are a poor judge of character, my dear.'

Adela was suddenly silent. She knew her brother. That mention of Jack meant that there was more going on than he was telling her.

'Very well, Clovis,' she said quietly. 'I know you have my best interests at heart.'

'Of course I do, my dear.' Clovis was surprised at how abruptly she had seen reason. 'Now, if you'll excuse me, I have to talk to some of the men about provisions for the drive.'

'Well,' said Adela sweetly, 'if your cook will allow me a corner in the kitchen, I think I might bake a pie, as I have no school today.'

Jack lay on the wooden plank-bed in the cell and tried to do a mental check of his injuries. His head ached as if he had been trampled by a horse. He could see out of one eye, the other was swollen shut. He ran the tips of his fingers gingerly across his face; it was swollen and sore down one side. There was blood in his nose and throat and his arms felt as if they had been wrenched out of their sockets. Out of the corner of his good eye he could see Bull Brown leaning back in his chair with his feet on the desk, idly reading a newspaper. A collection of flies buzzed with frustration, caught in a thick web in a corner of the window.

Sheriff Bull Brown's office was a small room with a door and windows on to the street. There were two more hard chairs opposite the desk and some faded posters on the walls. A Winchester was in a rack on the wall by the door. A brass spittoon and the cell keys on a heavy iron hoop lay on Bull's desk near his feet. The spittoon pinged, as Bull casually spat a ball of mucus and tobacco juice into it. The street door opened and Bill came in holding a wad of papers in his hand.

'Mornin', Sheriff.'

Bull grunted sourly. 'Whatcha got there?'

'Announcement papers,' Bill said. 'Look.' He handed one of the papers to Bull. 'One of the Diamondback boys passed these in at the store. Mr Blacklake says we gotta display 'em all over town.'

Bull swung his feet off the desk, picked up the keys and strode over to the cells. He clattered the keys along the cell bars. 'Wake up, drifter,' he sneered. 'You oughta hear this.'

'I'm listenin',' Jack said.

'Well, you better be. You listen good because if you don' understand what's on this here paper, you're likely to be locked in this jail till you rot.'

Bull cleared his throat and began to read slowly. 'Announcement of land claim. Acreage of land and buildings, formally known as "The Mission House", situated at the mouth of Bluebonnet Canyon, bordered by the ridge known as High Bluff to the north, open range belonging to the Diamondback Ranch to the south, east and west is hereby claimed and annexed to the same, by

Clovis Z. Blacklake, owner of the aforementioned Diamondback Ranch. This annexation is carried out in the absence of any deed of title to the property, in accordance with the Land Claims (Annexation Act) 1857. Any person or persons found on or interfering with this property will be deemed committing an act of trespass and be subject to the due process of law. Signed Clovis Z. Blacklake, proprietor and sole owner, Diamondback Ranch.'

Bull laughed. 'You understand that, drifter? Looks like you ain't got a reason to stay around here no more. Whenever it is Mr Blacklake decides you should be released from this pig pen, you gonna have to be on your way.'

'That ain't the law,' Jack said. 'And you know it.'

Bull stared contemptuously at him. 'I told you before. This here's the panhandle. I am the law and there ain't nothin' you can do about it. 'Course,' he grinned, 'if you do want to get out of this here jailhouse, bail in this town is set at a hundred dollars. You got a hundred dollars, drifter?'

He turned to Bill. 'Well, what are you waitin' for? If Mr Blacklake wants these on display, get to it!'

Clovis Blacklake sat astride a magnificent black stallion, his hand resting on the horn of his polished leather saddle. He clicked his tongue and whispered, 'Walk on, Devil.' The fine animal instantly responded, climbing a rise which gave a view over miles of open land and almost the whole of the Diamondback Ranch. Blacklake watched the cowboys at work below him.

The spring round-up was almost complete. Blacklake was waiting for a group of cowpunchers he had sent thirty miles south ostensibly to bring in strays, but in fact their job was to collect whatever longhorns they could, regardless of whom they belonged to, and add them to Blacklake's main herd. The drive north would have left the Diamondback before the owners realized their cattle were missing. Over the years, this technique of last-minute rustling had added considerably to Blacklake's profit.

It was a beautiful Texas scene. The wide-open sky was ice blue, buffalo grass rolled over mile after mile of the range. The whoops and hollas of the working men were carried on the warm morning breeze, as they circled and recircled the herd, separating longhorns which were not fit for the drive or steers which had not been branded. Dust clouds rose behind them.

Blacklake estimated the profit he was going to make. This was going to be his best year yet. Beeves which were worth four dollars a head on the panhandle would fetch forty dollars in the Kansas stockyards. He smiled with satisfaction. He was a successful man.

Back in town, at the stable, Moses finished brushing the horses. Since the pastor and his wife had died he had spent more time with horses than he had with people. Horses never let him down. His shotgun was leaning up against a stall nearby. Next to it was the Comanche knife he had found in the stable door early this morning. The difference today was that the knife had been lodged in the inside of the door. The young braves were getting surer of themselves.

Moses set a coffee pot to brew on a small fire in the yard at the back of the stable. The rich, dark smell always reminded him of his childhood at the mission house. There had always been a coffee pot percolating on the kitchen stove. He pictured the room, the red-and-white checkered tablecloth, the benches which the Pastor Joe had made, the thin panes of glass in the curtained windows, the wood fire with the heavy iron skillet hanging over it. He remembered Mary, the pastor's wife in her long apron, constantly cleaning the house. She scrubbed the floor until the boards were white, cleaned the windows with vinegar and water and polished the few pots she owned until they shone like the moon.

The pastor would spend his days tending the vegetable garden or making repairs to the house while he waited for the Comanche to come to Jesus, as he never doubted they would. The longer he waited, the more certain he became that his presence on the panhandle would bring the local bands of Indians to the Lord. He sang hymns in his sweet tenor voice as he worked. The house, which he had built with his own hands, always needed repairing. The cottonwood planks which made up the walls of the house were never true. They let in heat and dust in summer and the rain and cold in winter. Time after time Pastor Joe replaced them, but as soon as he did, they would warp and twist out of shape whatever the weather. Moses sat under the fig tree, basking in his reverie.

Suddenly, Moses' head was yanked backwards and there was a knife at his throat. A young Comanche brave stepped from behind him, while another held the knife. The chisel-faced young man glared at him in silent fury.

Hatred and cruelty danced in his eyes. His jet-black hair was in plaits like Moses's own. He wore a buffalo-hide shirt and pants, with decorated moccasins on his feet. He looked Moses up and down contemptuously and tapped the coffee pot with his foot, just enough to unbalance it and knock it over so that the coffee spilled into the fire and steam hissed into the air. He said something which Moses did not understand. The other Comanche let go of Moses's hair and took the knife away from his throat.

The first brave slipped into the stable and Moses heard him release one of the horses. The other brave stood between Moses and the door with his knife in his hand, ready to slash at him. Moses stood still, never taking his eyes off the knife, remembering he had left his scattergun inside. The first brave called out softly and the one with the knife followed him into the building. Moses dashed in after them. They were both at the front door, astride Goldie, Adela Blacklake's mare. One of them waved Moses's shotgun at him, from the back of the horse. They urged the horse on and lunged forward into a gallop out into the street and out of town. Moses watched helplessly. When they were a safe distance away, he heard them whoop to celebrate a victory.

Down the street a little, Silas Johnson had been washing the windows of his parents' hardware store.

'I saw the damnedest thing,' he said later to his brother Bill. 'I coulda sworn I saw two Injuns ride outa the stable. Bareback on the same horse.'

'Can't be,' Bill said. 'You think Moses been sellin' horses to the Injuns? What horse was it, anyways?'

'They was too far off when I seed 'em. Coulda been a chesnut.'

'Lemonade Lil's got a chesnut mare. Think that was the one?'

'Dunno. Only one way to find out. Let's get down there.'

'Damn me if Moses ain't sold Lil's mare to the Injuns.'

In the sheriff's office, Bull Brown finished reading his newspaper and tossed it idly down on the desk. The trouble with keeping the drifter locked up was that he was unable to use his hammock in the cell. The usual bail was a hundred dollars when someone was locked up, but no one ever paid it. Bull just released the prisoners either when they had sobered up or when he felt like it. But this drifter was different. He was going to have to wait for Blacklake to say when the cell door should be unlocked. The day was beginning to get hot again. Bull considered crossing the street to the saloon and sitting there awhile, if he couldn't snooze in the cell.

To Bull's surprise, the office door opened and Adela Blacklake stepped in carrying a wicker basket covered in a clean gingham cloth. Bull swung his boots off the desk and jumped up, almost knocking his chair over backwards.

'Why, Sheriff Brown, I can see you're hard at work protecting us poor townsfolk,' Adela said playfully. 'And we thank you for it, we surely do.'

As he often was by things Adela said, Bull was confused. He was unable to tell whether she meant it or whether she was teasing him in some way which was just out of reach of his comprehension. But she smiled so sweetly at him that he let it pass.

'Thank you, Miss Adela.'

'Now,' Adela said. 'I know how partial you are to my apple pie, Sheriff, so I thought I would bring one down to you. I had to come into town anyways to see Mrs Johnson at the store.' She pulled back the gingham cover of the basket to reveal a freshly baked apple pie. A fragrant cloud, scented with sugar, apples, cinnamon and cloves, filled the office.

Bull was completely taken aback. The woman he had been calling on for almost two years and who at times seemed not to take his compliments seriously had had a change of heart. For the first time, after all the posies and candy he had presented to her, she had brought him a present, one which she had made with her own hands and one which she knew was his particular favourite.

'Why, Miss Adela. . . .'

She appeared not to notice Jack who lay listening to all this on the cell bench. The flies buzzed again, struggling for freedom in the web at the corner of the window.

'There is just one thing,' Adela continued in a sing-song voice. 'I should like you to release this man. I know the town bail is a hundred dollars and I have come to pay it.'

Bull's face clouded. Adela was confusing him again. 'Miss Adela, I kin only do that on your brother's say so, you know that,' Bull whined.

'Now, Sheriff,' Adela said firmly. 'My money is as good as everyone else's, isn't it?'

'Why, yes but. . . .'

'Well then.' Adela set the basket down on the desk and

produced a roll of bills from beside the pie. She held them out to Bull.

'Miss Adela,' Bull said, eyeing the money, 'you know I can't. I must speak to your brother first.'

Adela insisted. 'I know this man, Nathan. There has been some misunderstanding. He is not the one to blame if there was a fight.'

Brown grinned. 'Now, that's sheriff's business, Adela. You don' know nothin' about that. I'm the law here. I'm the one to say who's to blame or not.'

He reached into the basket, slipped both hands under the pie and lifted it out. 'Now, I thank you kindly for this here pie, but you best put your money back in your purse. This drifter ain't goin' nowhere until your brother gives the say-so, even if you do want the rent for your back room.' Adela glanced hopelessly over at Jack.

As he placed the pie on the desk with deliberate carefulness, something which had been lying underneath it in the basket, caught Brown's eye. 'Hey, now. What's this here, Miss Adela?'

Bull picked up a small silver derringer and held it out to Adela 'What you doin' with this here little popgun? You sure as hell ain't gonna catch no outlaws with this!' Bull chuckled at his own joke. He held the gun flat in the palm of his great hand to emphasize its smallness and took his own sidearm out of its holster with his other hand for comparison. 'Now this here's a Remington, Army model. I had it since the war. Know how I came by it? Came across a Yankee officer boy one day. He was lyin' on the ground in the woods up around Dry Wood Creek, Vernon County, Missouri, groanin' an' callin' out for his mama. He'd fallen off his horse and busted his back. He was wounded anyways. His gun was right there in his holster so I took it and shot him right there and then with his own gun. Shot him right in the head. Kept the Remington as a souvenir, right to this day. Fine gun it is, even if it belonged to a damn Yankee.'

He turned and pointed the Remington at Jack and squinted along the sights. 'I could blow his brains out with this, if I had a mind to.' He laughed contemptuously and held up the derringer. 'Bullet from this little lady's toy wouldn't even make a dent in his thick skull.'

He slipped the Remington back into its holster and held the derringer just out of Adela's reach. He leered at her. 'Bein' the officer of the law, an' as it's my sworn duty to protect the citizens of this town, I'm thinkin' I should keep hold of this here dangerous weapon, Miss Adela. I don' think I should let a fine lady like yourself be walkin' about with a handgun in your basket.'

'My brother bought me that gun for my own protection, Mr Brown,' Adela said tartly. 'Will you please give it back to me.'

Bull continued to wave the derringer at Adela, just out of her reach. Adela put up with this taunting and stared at him, stony-faced. Then she made a grab for the gun. Bull's hand closed over it to keep it from her. There was a loud report and a bellow of pain from Bull. Blood sprayed over the desk. The derringer clattered to the floor and the tip of Bull's little finger rolled beside it.

Bull clasped the stump of his finger with his other hand, howling and cursing in agony. 'You ain't supposed to walk around with the hammer cocked,' he screamed,

73

blood oozing through his fingers.

Adela was white-faced with shock. After a moment, she collected her thoughts. 'Now you just sit down, Sheriff.' She guided Bull towards his chair. 'You just sit there for a moment and you keep the pressure on that wound to stop the bleeding. Then when you're feeling calm enough, you walk over to the saloon and get Charlie to give you some water to wash it in. Then you tie it up good and tight with this'. She lifted her skirt and tore a strip off the bottom of her cotton petticoat.

'You understand me, Sheriff?' Bull nodded, grimacing with pain. 'But for the moment, you just sit there and keep the pressure on that wound.' She scooped up the derringer from the floor, took the bunch of keys from the table, walked over to Jack's cell and unlocked the door. She left the roll of bills on the desk. Bull gave a moan of protest and then slumped back in his chair as Adela and Jack slipped out of the office and into the street.

7

Taking care to keep out of sight behind the row of buildings, Jack returned to the schoolhouse to collect his guns. He then headed for the lumber yard by the same route to order some hardwood stakes to shore up the sides of the well. He tried to call in at the bank to collect the deeds to the mission property, but it was closed. He knew this was not a good sign, as someone who lived by the company rulebook as closely as Clarence Fayette did would never shut the bank during opening hours unless something was wrong. Adela walked up the middle of the street to Johnson's Hardware.

At the lumber yard, the foreman promised to have hardwood stakes and crosspieces cut and delivered to the old mission that afternoon. He did not register any surprise at the request. He also said he was expecting a delivery of pine boards from Kansas via Dodge City. 'You'll be needin' some o' them if you're fixin' up the mission. Place is fallin' down, ain't it?' Jack said he would be back when the delivery came in.

As usual, the stables were immaculate. Moses had swept

and washed the floor that morning. The horses had been exercised, brushed, fed and watered. He was clearly nervous and told Jack about the braves stealing Adela Blacklake's mare. He told him the two deputies had come round and tried to make out he had sold the horse to the Comanche, but had refused, when he asked them, to search the place for money or some kind of payment. They had said that they would report him to the sheriff and Mr Blacklake and that he would be run out of town.

Jack and Moses saddled up and headed out to the mission. Jack couldn't be certain, but he didn't think anyone had seen them leave.

The bottom of the well was covered by four inches of water, the result of a steady seepage overnight. Jack scrambled down into it to inspect their handiwork. He took off his shirt, soaked it and held it up to his bruised face. He scooped up handfuls of the cool, silver liquid and drank as if it were wine. He filled his hat and passed it up for Moses to try.

The two men agreed that they would wait until the hardwood stakes arrived and they could shore up the sides properly before they dug any deeper, to avoid a collapse. They turned their attention to the house instead. Moses was full of excitement and described to Jack how the place had looked when the Minister and his wife were alive. Now, it was a wreck.

The veranda had fallen down and many of the wall- and floor-planks were bowed out of shape and would have to be renewed. The window glass was broken and the door was hanging off its hinges. Some of the roof shingles had come adrift and lay scattered on the ground. The timber frame was still true, though, and the stone-built chimney stood firm.

They started with the roof. Jack took off his gunbelt and set it down behind the door inside the house. Moses collected up the shingles and found an old ladder the minister had made lying discarded at the back of the building. Jack climbed up and hammered the shingles back into place. From the roof, he noticed that the same Comanche on horseback was watching them again from the bluff above them. They worked on all morning.

After a while they realized that if they took the bowed planks out, sawed off the most twisted parts and nailed them back in a kind of patchwork, they would be able to make do with most of the timber they had. It wouldn't look beautiful, but they would hardly need to cut any more. They set to, Moses starting at one end of a plank and Jack at the other, working towards each other, easing the nails out carefully so they could reuse them. Moses dragged up an old cottonwood trunk for Jack to use as a bench for the sawing and handed the nails and pieces of board to him as he hammered them into place.

By mid-afternoon they had run out of nails and the timbers to shore up the well had not arrived. Moses said he would ride the mile back into town to collect nails and call in at the lumber yard. Jack risked being locked up again if Bull or his deputies saw him. If the hardwood stakes were cut ready, Moses would tie them on to Jack's mule at the stable and bring them out with him. As the lumber yard was next to the stable and the foreman knew Moses well, there was no reason to think there would be any trouble. Before he left, Moses lowered the bucket into the well and brought up a cool drink for them both. 'Our water,' he said, beaming with pride.

It was a searing hot day. July heat in May. Heat shimmered over the land and the sky was as hard as glass. Jack sat in the shade of one of the cottonwoods and watched Moses head off across the plain. He wetted his shirt again and held it on the aching bruises on the side of his face. Eventually Moses turned into a speck in the distance and disappeared. Jack scooped handfuls of water from the bucket beside him and drank, leaned back against the trunk of the cotton wood and pulled his hat down over his eyes.

Sometime later, unsure whether he was awake or dreaming, Jack heard a horse whinny. He jerked himself awake, expecting to see Moses. Instead, loosely tethered to the old veranda rail of the house was a fine chestnut mare. He recognized her immediately as Goldie, Adela Blacklake's horse. Moses had pointed her out in the stable on the day he arrived. Jack walked round the property, but there was no one about. He checked inside the house, round the back and behind the stand of cotton trees. No-one. But high up on the bluff, the Comanche on horseback waved to him. He raised his arm high and seemed to draw an arc in the sky. Then he turned his horse abruptly and disappeared over the other side of the hill.

Jack looked the chestnut over. She was just as well-looked-after as when Moses had charge of her in the livery stable. She stood calm and unconcerned as Jack held the bucket filled with well-water for her to drink. He gently patted her neck and she flicked her long, dark mane in reply. Jack untied her, led her into the shade of the stand of cottonwoods where his own horse stood and looped her reins round a branch. He kept checking the skyline to see if the Comanche had returned, but it was empty. Puzzled, he wondered whether Moses would know what was behind the sudden return of the horse.

While he waited for Moses, Jack set about filling his time by starting to take up the most warped floorboards. It was difficult work. The oblong heads of the nails were buried deep into the wood. To get them out without bending them, so they could be reused, or without gouging holes in the boards, was almost impossible. After an hour, he heard the sound of horses.

He jumped up, again expecting to see Moses. As he stepped outside, he faced the barrel of a Winchester pointing straight at his head. The Johnson boys, sporting their deputy stars, were sitting on their horses staring straight at him. Silas had the Winchester trained on him and Bill had him covered with a .44. Jack's hand instinctively went for his Peacemaker, only to find he wasn't wearing his gunbelt.

Silas saw this and laughed. Bull Brown appeared from round the side of the house on his horse, also covering Jack with a Winchester.

'You're comin' with us,' he snapped. Jack's eyes rested on the blood-soaked bandage round the little finger of his right hand. 'I knew you was gonna be trouble first time I saw you. I shoulda shot you right there an' then.' He spat a stream of tobacco juice through his teeth, fury blazing in his eyes. 'Mr Blacklake wants to see you. That's why we've had to ride out here in this damn heat to git you. So you get on your horse and you ride real slow back towards town and we'll be ten paces right behind you. Know why that is, drifter? That's so if you ride too fast or too slow or you do any damn thing we don' like, all three of us kin shoot you in the back. An' I kin tell you, right now there ain't nothin' I'd enjoy better.'

Jack mounted his horse and without speaking or looking at Bull or the deputies started out for town at a walking pace.

'Damn if that ain't Miss Adela Blacklake's horse,' Bill said, noticing the bay tethered beside Jack's. 'What's that doing out here?'

'I'll take her,' Bull said. 'You boys keep him covered.'

Clovis Blacklake stood with his back to the room staring out of the window, which overlooked some of the ranch buildings. Jack waited in front of his vast, polished desk waiting for him to be good enough to turn round. Silas had a gun pressed into the small of his back. Bull leaned indolently against a wall. Clovis took his time, seeming to be intent on watching the activity of the ranch below. At last he turned to face Jack.

Clovis's sour, sallow face was fixed in a sneer of contempt. His black hair was greased back and parted precisely in the centre. The tips of his moustache were carefully waxed and pointed upwards beside his narrow beak of a nose. His thin lips were open, revealing a gold tooth. He wore a black riding-jacket, immaculate white shirt and a thin, black bow tie. His black waistcoat was decorated with gold thread. He wore a black polished-leather gunbelt with a pearl-handled Colt at each hip. His pants were pressed and his black riding-boots shone like lakewater under moonlight. He looked like Satan come to the panhandle.

'I bin hearin' about you,' he said softly, 'an' to tell the truth, I ain't bin likin' what I heard.' He paused to take a fat cigar from the silver box on his desk. He rolled it between his fingers thoughtfully and held it under his nose, closed his eyes and sniffed the aroma of the tobacco leaves. He tossed the cigar over to Bull, who lurched forward to catch it. Blacklake selected another for himself from the box, clipped off the end with a pair of silver clippers attached to the chain of his fob watch and lit it.

'Somebody told me you bin helping that Injun dig a well out on the old mission. This was an error on your part, mister. I know Moses thinks the mission belongs to him. But it don't. I am a plain-speakin' man and I'm tellin' you, that is my land. I have laid claim to it within the law.'

'It ain't no legal claim,' Jack said firmly. 'That land belongs to Moses, inherited by will from the pastor.'

Blacklake laughed. 'So you're the lawyer now? Evidence is what lawyers rely on. Where's the evidence? Where is this will? Where are the deeds?' Blacklake leaned towards him confidentially. 'That Injun can't hardly read his own name. How does he know he's mentioned in a will?'

'The pastor told him,' Jack said calmly, 'before he deposited the deeds in the bank.'

Blacklake sat down in his chair and looked at Jack with amusement. 'What kinda fool are you? Takin' the word of an illiterate Injun. What're you tryin' to do?'

'Tryin' to do what's right, is all,' Jack said.

'What's right?' Blacklake repeated. 'What's right? You are a damn fool. There ain't no right in this. This here's the panhandle. This place belongs to me. I built it. I own it. Don't you come "what's right" with me.' Blacklake exhaled a column of blue cigar smoke. 'That Injun was quite content workin' at the stable till you came and put ideas in his head. Made him think he could do things it weren't intended for him to do. You've come here and interrupted the natural order of things, mister. An' I can't be lettin' you do that.'

'Let me have 'im, boss,' Bull said, excited. 'Let me take 'im outside. The boys'll hold him an' I'll plough 'im like a field.' Blacklake ignored him.

'Now,' he continued coldly, 'that's bad enough, but that ain't all. I know that my sister, out of the goodness of her heart, has let you stay at the schoolhouse. I am not surprised by this because she is a good-hearted woman who is disposed to look kindly on stray dogs, people who are sick, men who drift into town an' suchlike. She has a pitying nature and takes pity on people who seem to need help.' Cigar smoke wreathed around Blacklake, giving the impression that he was burning. His gold tooth glinted as he spoke.

'I. . . .' Jack began. Clovis held up a hand to silence him.

'Mr Blacklake don' like to be interrupted,' Silas hissed behind Jack's ear, jabbing the pistol barrel into his kidneys.

'I know that she took pity on you,' Blacklake continued, 'an' I ain't surprised. It's how she is. My sister is a single woman an' is vulnerable to someone who might want to

82

take advantage of her.' He paused. His voice seemed to lower by an octave and come from somewhere deep inside him. 'I understand that my sister took it upon herself to pay your bail.' Jack felt Blacklake's eyes bore into him. 'I understand that my sister paid the bail of a man whom she had shown a kindness to and who turned out to be a lawbreaker and a common criminal.' His voice creaked like a rusty hinge and his cigar smoke hung in the air.

'Whatcha want me to do with him, boss?' Bull said.

'Quiet,' Blacklake snapped. 'My sister may be misguided, but I most certainly do not wish to upset her.' He turned to Jack. 'You will stay away from Miss Adela. You will ride out to the mission and stay there tonight. Tomorrow you will fill in the well you dug, as it might be a danger to the steers when the cattle drive goes through there. Then you will get on your horse, take your mule and you will leave. I don' care which way you go, but you will leave the panhandle. I am a deliberate man, mister. There ain't no one who don't do what I say.' He waved his hand to indicate that Bull and the deputies should take Jack away. Silas didn't miss the opportunity to jab his gunbarrel viciously into Jack's kidneys as he shoved him out through the door.

'We gotta get rid of this Indian someday soon,' Clovis muttered, half to himself, 'jus' to tidy things up.'

'I hear you, boss,' Bull smirked. 'This drifter. Whyn't you let me take care of him? Ain't no one gonna miss a drifter.'

'I'm not havin' nothin' happenin' which causes no grief to Adela. Best thing that can happen is that he jus' rides on outa town all nice 'n quiet, so we kin forget about him. I think we've given him enough encouragement for that.'

The deputies escorted Jack to the gates of the Diamondback Ranch with their six-shooters trained on him all the way. A huge, polished-wood sign hung over the gates carved in the shape of a Diamondback rattler with its markings painted in black and brown.

'We gonna wait here for the sheriff,' Silas sneered, 'so you jus' ride on out to the mission an' get to fillin' in that well, jus' like Mr Blacklake said, yuh hear?'

Bill giggled. 'If he don', Silas, you 'n me kin give him another whippin'.'

'Ain't that the truth,' Silas observed coldly.

Jack ignored the taunts and encouraged his horse into a trot. He didn't look back.

8

Spirited laughter and children's chatter greeted Jack as he opened the schoolroom door. A crowd of little'uns pressed round the teacher's desk as Adela distributed homemade lemonade and biscuits she had baked herself. It was break-time.

'Miss, miss,' one little boy said, tugging at Adela's skirt. 'Miss, there's a man.'

Adela looked up, peered short-sightedly across the room and then realized who it was. 'Welcome,' she said, beaming. 'As you can see, you've caught us at the most important part of the morning. Can I offer you a glass of lemonade, Mr Just? I know Jimmy here won't mind giving his up for a visitor.'

Jimmy, the boy who had first noticed Jack, stood beside Adela, his fist clenched round the handle of a tin cup. He looked momentarily horrified at the possible loss of his lemonade. Adela patted him on the head.

'Don't worry, son,' Jack grinned. 'I ain't thirsty.'

Jimmy smiled with relief and quickly gulped down his drink before anyone else could lay claim to it.

'Right, children, you can play outside for fifteen minutes,' Adela announced. As one, the class swept out of the schoolroom door on a wave of high spirits, leaving Jack and Adela alone.

'I've come to collect my things,' Jack said simply. He told Adela about the meeting with her brother. 'It's best if I stay out at the mission for a while. Maybe he'll calm down an' me an' Moses can work on the place without no trouble.' Jack spoke the words to reassure Adela, but as he spoke he did not believe what he was saying. He knew Blacklake wanted him gone and he knew Bull Brown would like to get his deputies to kill him while he watched from a safe distance.

'I'll speak to Clovis,' Adela said, her jaw thrust out. 'He'll listen to me. He's used to ordering people about, all the ranch hands. You must understand, Jack, he has to be like that. He means it for the best, I know he does. He wants to protect me. But he cannot dictate whom I have or don't have under the schoolhouse roof.'

Adela was used to making excuses for her brother. Storekeepers sometimes complained to her that the rents were too high; ranch hands complained that the food was poor on the Diamondback and that while they had been hired as cattlemen, they often had to spend their time quarrying stone up at Bluebonnet Canyon for the boss's new ranch house for no extra pay. And she had tended the bruised and broken faces of the cowboys who had been beaten by Bull Brown's deputies, in her brother's name. It was clear to her that sometimes Clovis could be a little overbearing. But no-one knew about his years of hard work and struggle like she did. She felt she saw him from the inside, while others just saw the Boss of the Diamondback. She knew that Clovis, who had achieved so much, was her protector. He would never let harm come to her. And as her eyesight got steadily worse, she needed him.

Jack collected his few belongings from the back room where he had been staying.

'Don't judge Clovis harshly, Jack,' Adela said. 'In his own way he's a great man. Just a little hasty at times.'

At first, Jack couldn't see Moses. The stables were fuller than he had known them. Horses were crowded in two, sometimes three to a stall. More were tethered to the rail outside. Moses was in the shadows at the back of the stable, filling water troughs for the new arrivals.

He broke off from his work as soon as he saw Jack. The hardwood stakes to shore up the well's sides should have been delivered by now, he said. He could come on out to the mission as soon as he got through here. Though he wasn't sure when that would be exactly, as people kept arriving.

'This is the first time I ever had anything that was mine,' Moses said. Jack hesitated before telling him about Blacklake's orders to him to move out.

'What you gonna do?'

'Two types of men in the world,' Jack said. 'One type only takes on a fight he knows he can win.'

'What's the other type?' Moses asked.

'Hell,' Jack said. 'The ones who take on a fight anyways.'

Moses smiled. 'And which one are you?'

'Guess I'm just about to find out,' Jack said 'Guess you are too.'

87

'I got a lot to do here,' Moses said, indicating the horses tethered two to a stall. He avoided Jack's eye. 'Lot o' people come into town to see the Chinaman fight.'

'Guess so. See you got Adela Blacklake's horse back.'

'The sheriff brought it in,' Moses said. 'He said I was to take special care of it.' Then he added, 'I always do that. He didn't have to tell me.'

Jack took the mule from the stable and led him out into the sunlight. He mounted his own horse. 'You get that scattergun back?' he asked Moses.

'Nope.'

'Here,' Jack pulled his Winchester out of its saddle holster and tossed it down to Moses.

'Ain't never fired one o' these,' Moses said, looking the rifle over.

Jack grinned. 'You won't have no trouble with it. Works the same as a scattergun. You just pull the trigger an' if you're lucky, you hit what you're aimin' at.'

He tugged at the reins of his horse and clicked his tongue for the animal to walk on.

'You gonna fill in the well?' Moses called after him. 'Like Blacklake says?'

Jack raised his hand to salute goodbye. But he didn't answer.

Despite Bull's threats, the well was just as Jack had left it. The only visitor to the mission had been the lumber yard cart. Its tracks were clearly visible in the dust and there was a pile of hardwood stakes neatly stacked beside the well. Jack peered down into the hole. It looked like water was continuing to seep in. It could be as much as a foot deep now. To support a homestead here, the well would have to be a great deal deeper, or maybe a second well would have to be dug.

Jack checked out the rest of the property. His gunbelt and pair of Peacemakers were still behind the door inside. He buckled the belt on, still thinking about the well. He walked round the back of the building. The rope, bucket and pile of tools were just where he had left them. From Moses's description of what the place was like in the pastor's day, the stream which flowed through the canyon and which had mysteriously dried up must have been a steady source of water all year round, even in summer. The pastor and his wife had never needed to dig a well.

Lowering the bucket, Jack could see that the seeping water was already causing the sides of the well to begin to crumble. He drank long, deep, cooling draughts from the bucket, letting the water spill generously over himself and soak into his shirt. It made him feel rich in a place where there was only the poverty of baked earth and the dry bark of the cottonwood trees. He fetched the ladder and a lump-hammer, threw down a few stakes into the well, climbed down and set to work, keeping his gunbelt within easy reach, hanging from one of the rungs.

It was difficult working in the cramped conditions. Even though the floor of the well was wet, it still required great force to knock the stakes in. Jack worked on until his back and shoulders burned like fire, loosening the cottonwood planks and tossing them out of the well and driving in the hardwoods to replace them. After two solid hours in the hole, Jack climbed out to take a break, taking care to bring his gunbelt up with him. He found a piece of beef jerky in his saddle-bag and washed it down with crystal-clear well water, leaning back against a cottonwood. Looking up to the bluff, he saw the same Comanche on horseback, watching him.

Huge banks of cloud gathered in the sky to the east. The colour began to deepen in the landscape after the bleaching light of the afternoon. There were only a couple of hours of daylight left. It looked to Jack as though Moses would come out to join him in the morning. Jack got a fire going and collected a pile of brushwood to keep it in through the night, then he went back down the well to hammer in the last few stakes.

When he climbed the ladder again it was almost dark. To the west, the dying sun left a splash of pink-and-purple light over the horizon. Wind was getting up and a fork of lightning flickered across the sky a hundred miles or more to the south. Jack built up the fire and put his coffee on to brew. He undid his bedroll and laid it out beside the fire. He had spent so many nights like this, he was almost more used to it than he was to sleeping in a bed. He made the gunbelt his pillow. In the morning, he thought, after he had finished nailing the crosspieces to the hardwood, he would ride up the canyon to find out why the creek had run dry. Though in the back of his mind, he knew.

Dreams flickered around Jack all night. Scenes from years ago, from the mountains and from the war were confused with him digging the well. Endlessly digging and never finding water. And everywhere the dreams took him, he seemed to be watched over by the Comanche on horseback. Jack awoke troubled and tired before first light. He rebuilt the fire from the glowing embers and made coffee. He wrapped himself tight in his bedroll. The sharp morning air chilled his bones.

It took Jack longer than he'd expected to fix the crosspieces. It was mid-morning by the time he had finished. There was about eighteen inches of water in the bottom of the well now, but the hardwood stakes had been forced inward by the weight of wet earth during the night. Another day without the support of the crosspieces, and the whole thing would collapse. Jack jammed the wooden struts in tight and nailed them fast. By the time he had finished the well could have withstood an earthquake.

As he climbed the ladder again, he saw a lone rider in the distance, approaching from the direction of town. Jack took it to be Moses and was pleased he had finished shoring up the well sides, so he could show his work to his friend. Moses would be useful company too, riding up the creek, if the Comanches were watching.

As the figure draw nearer, Jack realized that the rider was Adela. She was balancing a basket in front of her on the saddle.

' 'Mornin',' she said brightly, handing the basket down to Jack. 'I haven't ridden out here in a while. I used to come every week when Mary and Pastor Joe were here. I brought you some breakfast.'

'Thank you kindly. Good to have some company.'

'Where's Moses? Isn't he out here too?'

'Last I saw of him was in the stable yesterday. Place was jammed with horses. Said he'd come out here as soon as he could.'

'I didn't see him this morning,' Adela said. 'Had to unhitch Goldie myself. I got one of the boys from the

91

Diamondback who was in town to saddle her up for me. The stable was full to overflowing though. Horses out back, out front, three to a stall inside. Everyone's come into town to see this Chinaman fight. Lord knows why. I spend half my day breaking up fights in the school yard. It's just little boys showing off. This prize fight is just little boys who have grown into big men but still stayed little boys inside, in my opinion.'

Jack smiled and helped her down from her horse.

'Besides that,' Adela continued, 'I heard some Indians took Goldie. They do whatever they can to torment poor Moses. He's an easy target for the young braves.'

Adela walked cautiously round the well, peering into it. 'My, my, you have dug a long way. And have you reached water yet?'

'Purest there is,' Jack said. 'Trouble is, there ain't enough of it. Not for a place this size.' He rinsed his tin mug in the bucket and proudly scooped a drink for her to try.

'I could make some coffee,' Jack suggested hesitantly.

'This water's fine,' Adela smiled. 'Now, I want you to see what I've brought you.' She sat on a cottonwood log and started to unpack the basket. 'I roasted a chicken, there's bread and there's pie.' She unwrapped each item in turn to show Jack and then wrapped them up again in clean white cloths.

'Mighty nice of you, Adela, I don' know what to say.'

'Jack Just, I do believe you're blushing,' Adela teased him. 'If my old eyes worked better, I'm sure I could see you were.'

'I'm just grateful for such nice food, ma'am. Any man

92

would be. I been surviving on well-water, coffee and beef jerky.'

Jack took the basket, tore a leg off the chicken and a piece off the loaf and ate. 'Did you speak to your brother?'

'He says the mission is part of the Diamondback. He's claimed it. He wants to run the drive through here.'

'You know the pastor left the mission to Moses in his will?' Jack said.

'I know,' Adela said anxiously, 'but you got to understand, Jack. This is the panhandle. Papers and lawyer's deeds don't mean what they do back East.'

'What's right and what's wrong means the same anywheres. It ain't to do with lawyers' papers, Adela.'

'I'll keep trying,' Adela said. 'He may come round after the drive. That's all he's thinking about now. You can't blame him for that. He may let you and Moses live here and work on the place after the drive passes through.'

'He wants me gone, Adela,' Jack said quietly. 'He wants Moses workin' in the stables and beddin' down in a horse's stall. That ain't no way to live.'

'When he finds out you've improved the place, dug a well. When he knows that, he'll change his mind.' Adela took off her thick spectacles and wiped the dust off them with an embroidered handkerchief. 'I know he will.'

Jack changed the subject abruptly. 'That food was mighty fine, Miss Adela. You rear that chicken yourself?'

'I surely did. That was a corn-fed chicken. Not raised on scraps. One of my best birds. And I baked the bread.'

'Delicious,' Jack said. 'I'm gonna keep the basket lowered halfway down the well where it's cool and where the ants ain't gonna get at it. Me an' Moses'll finish the

93

rest when he gets here.'

Jack told her of his plan to ride up the canyon, and told her about the Comanche who appeared on the ridge and watched them. Adela smiled. 'That's Moses's brother. His name's Noconah. He turns up from time to time when the Comanche are back in this part of the panhandle. He'll have been the one who returned Goldie. Moses says he likes to keep an eye on him. He's his elder brother. He hasn't forgotten Moses, even if the rest of them have. The young braves dare each other to ride up to the stables and torment poor Moses sometimes. Noconah tries to protect him.'

Jack listened intently. 'Maybe Noconah wants his brother to rejoin the Comanche?'

'Moses thinks he does. But he can't talk to him. Moses hardly knows any Comanche, because they gave him away when he was a baby. Noconah doesn't speak English.' Adela stood up. 'I should be getting back, before Clovis misses me. It wouldn't be favourable to you if he knew I was here.'

'Do you want me to ride with you?' Jack said.

'Why Mr Just, I do declare, you are a proper Southern gentleman.' Adela burst into a fit of giggles. 'No, Jack,' she said, pulling herself together. 'Even if my poor old eyes can't see, Goldie knows the way.'

9

After Adela had headed back to town, Jack strapped on his gunbelt, tied a pick and shovel on to his saddle-bags and set off up the canyon. Some quarrying had been done at the mouth of the canyon, great hunks of rock had been smashed carelessly out of the canyon wall. Layers of red rock reared each side of him as he carefully guided his horse over the stony riverbed. Since the stream had dried, nothing grew there apart from a few, isolated clumps of feather grass high up on ledges where enough moisture had collected to sustain them. The heat of the sun bounced back off the rock walls at first. But the further Jack rode, the narrower the canyon became and the more it was filled with shadows. He seemed to be riding right into the landscape itself. This canyon was a crack in the high plains and showed what was underneath them, layer upon layer of hard, red rock, boulders, stones and dust.

Jack dismounted after a couple of miles, fearing that his horse might slip and break a leg on the unforgiving ground. He noticed the way the bedrock at his feet was worn away by the imprint of flowing water and the great quantity of stone that had been brought down in its wake. The stream had once been fast-flowing here and would have brought life to this dead land. No wonder, he thought, the pastor had picked the mouth of the canyon for his homestead.

Progress on foot was slow. After another hour Jack considered leaving his horse and walking on up the canyon by himself, carrying the pick and shovel over his shoulder. He wondered too about what Adela had said. Was it possible that she could persuade Blacklake to let Moses rebuild the mission? And if Moses could stay there, then Jack himself could too. The more work he and Moses did on the mission, the more Adela would defend it and the harder it would be for Blacklake to tear it down.

If the stream was flowing again, Jack thought, Blacklake would find a way of turning that to his advantage too. Maybe the mission could be a stopping-off point on the drive for cattle from the southern part of the round-up, before they climbed the ridge and headed north on the long trail over the high plains. All this was possible, Jack thought, except for one thing. If truth be told, Clovis Blacklake wanted him dead.

At a fork in the canyon, about a mile further on, Jack found the dam. Blacklake had had this built to cut off water from the mission and make the place uninhabitable. It had been strongly built too. A wall of pine logs, ten feet high and lined with clay, was shored up by boulders and stone. The dam was far higher and stronger than anything required by the flow of water. It had taken many men days to build. The water came from a spring in the rock side here and now formed a pool behind the dam, before making a new course down the fork in the canyon that ran to the east. Jack knew where this came out. He had seen it on his journey south. The diverted water would eventually irrigate the grassless desert which formed the part of the Diamondback property east of town.

In the dust round the pool were the tracks of deer and cottontail rabbits. Hoofprints were there too. There was a twisting path down the steep side of the canyon. The Comanche had been coming down to water their horses. Jack led his own horse to drink and inspected the rock supporting the dam wall and wondered where to start.

He untied the heavy pickaxe from his saddle and used it to try and lever the smaller boulders away from the dam wall. They were jammed in so tight, Jack was afraid he would break the shaft of the pick if he carried on. He set to trying to break the redrock boulder instead. It was hard, slow work. Even in the shade of the canyon the temperature was climbing again. Sweat poured off him. The steady blows of the pick did little more than chip away at the rock. Occasionally, a bigger piece would come loose.

After an hour, Jack put down the pick. He had made almost no progress. Rock dust and a pile of chippings lay at his feet. He filled his canteen from the pool, drank deeply and after allowing himself a few minutes' rest, started work again. He found his rhythm and worked with regular, accurate blows at trying to split the boulder. Eventually it happened. A crack suddenly ran across the rock and it seemed to have split completely in half. But the two halves were wedged in so tightly that Jack still couldn't pull or lever them out. He started to drive the pickaxe in at an angle to free a segment of the boulder to give him

97

leverage. The clay lining and the wall of timber holding in the water behind the rock was so strongly bedded in that the surface of the pool barely trembled at his blows.

'Whatcha doin' down there? You buildin' it up or breakin' it down?'

The voice came from high above. Jack looked up. Against the sunlight all he could see was the silhouette of a man's head in a plainsman's hat, peering over the cliff edge. Jack put down his pick. The voice had interrupted his working rhythm, but he was glad of a break anyway.

'Guess I'm pullin' it down. Rerouting the stream,' Jack called.

The silhouette of a second head appeared beside the first. No hat this time, but the man had what Jack took to be a Comanche pigtail.

'Looks like it's got you beat, mister.'

'I ain't given up yet.'

'Looks like you could do with a hand anyways.'

The heads disappeared. Then a couple of minutes later, two figures came scrambling down the zigzag path to the pool, sending a shower of dust and stones ahead of them. They picked their way round the side of the water, jumped down off the dam and stood beside Jack.

The first man was tall and thin as a stick of willow. He had a pinched, unshaven face with a thin line of moustache over his top lip. His eyes twinkled with amusement and he seemed as if he was just about to break out laughing. He was dressed with the faded grandeur of a dishevelled undertaker. Black jacket, grey, striped pants, a dirty white shirt and a dusty, black, wide-brimmed hat. He held out his hand to Jack and announced grandly

'Luther T. Pope, entrepreneur, at your service.'

The second man was a mountain. Six feet six high, Jack reckoned, huge, muscular shoulders and arms and a vast barrel-like belly. He wore baggy black pants, a black waistcoat and his long hair was knotted into a pigtail. A small black skullcap perched on his head. Jack recognized him immediately. This was the Chinese prize fighter. Like his companion, there was good humour written across the Chinaman's big, scarred face. The two of them looked as if finding Jack in the canyon was the funniest thing that had happened to them in days. The Chinaman held out his hand, just as Pope had done. 'Lee Yoo,' he said, introducing himself.

Jack shook hands with them both.

'This looks like a mighty strong dam to me,' Pope said.

'Sure is,' said Jack.

Pope caught the Chinaman's eye. 'This your dam, mister, if you don't mind me askin'?'

'Nope, it ain't,' Jack said. Again, Pope and the Chinaman exchanged glances.

Pope seemed to consider. 'The owner of this here dam, he knows you're takin' it down, right?'

'Nope.'

Pope coughed to disguise a chuckle. 'Well, whatcha doin' it for?' Pope and Lee Yoo clutched their sides and howled with laughter.

'Man who built the dam,' Jack said matter-of-factly, 'stole the water from my property.'

Peals of laughter from Pope and Lee echoed up the canyon.

Lee Yoo pulled himself together first. 'That ain't right.'

'Sure ain't. Now,' Pope said, addressing Jack, 'how's about we do a trade?'

'What?'

'We've got a wagon half a mile back with a broke axle. You've got a dam needs takin' down. Whyn't we help each other out? You got a place near here somewhere. You must have a piece of timber we could use as an axle, strong enough to get us into town so's we can have it fixed. You help us with that and ol' Lee here'll have that dam down quicker than a fork o' lightnin' in a spring storm. What d'ya say?'

Pope grinned at Jack.

'Who's gonna go first?' Jack said cautiously.

'Flip of a coin will decide,' Pope announced. He took a half-dollar from his jacket pocket and turned it over in the palm of his hand to show Jack both sides were different.

'OK,' Jack said. 'Heads it's the dam first.'

'I ain't a gamblin' man,' Pope said. 'But I do like to flip a coin. Makes things kinda exciting.'

'Odds is fifty-fifty,' Lee added. ' 'Course, if you make it best of three, odds is nine to one.'

'Hear that?' Pope winked at Jack. 'Ol' Lee's sharp as a tack.'

Pope flipped the coin high in the air, caught it and slapped it down on the back of his hand. He chuckled and drew his hand away with a dramatic flourish. The three of them peered down at the coin. 'Heads it is.'

To Jack's amazement, Lee Yoo started to pull boulders out of the dam with his bare hands. He worked until the whole pile of stone supporting the timber wall was loosened and water was beginning to trickle through.

100

What had taken him all morning to accomplish was dwarfed by Lee Yoo in the space of half an hour. Pope stood aside and let Lee Yoo work.

'Never seen no one stronger,' Pope said. 'An' I never seen no one add a column of figures faster than him neither.'

'Really?' Jack said.

'An' he don' use his fingers to count on,' Pope added proudly. 'He can calculate the odds in a poker game quick as you like. See, me 'n him's a team. He's the brains and the muscle, I'm the entrepreneur an' I drive the wagon.'

Jack and Pope sat on a rock, watching Lee Yoo hurl boulders away from the wall as if his life depended on it.

'I met ol' Lee in a saloon in San Francisco. He used to play poker when he wasn't workin' on the railroad. Damn near always won too. One night he cleaned up, then all the guys jumped him because they'd lost. Said he was cheatin', but he wasn't. Ol' Lee don't have to cheat. He can win fair and square without cheatin'.' Pope grinned at the memory. 'He was pickin' guys up and throwin' them through the door and out into the street like they was flour sacks. After I seed that I decided to quit the patent medicine business I was in at the time and go into the prizefight business with of Lee. Turned out pretty well too. Me 'n him gets along together good.'

'I can see that,' Jack said. His friendly interest in what he was being told encouraged Pope to keep talking.

' 'Course, being an entrepreneur, I put a few stories out about Lee an' how strong he is to create interest in the fight. When we get to a town, I tell people things like when he worked for the California railroad, he used to pick up

101

a rail under each arm, or the reason he's got such quick reactions is he eats raw snakes. 'Course he don' never eat raw snakes, he eats rice mostly. You'd be surprised what people'll believe. Don't do harm to no one. Jus' creates interest.'

'I'd be interested, if I heard that,' Jack reflected.

We got a prize fight comin' up near here,' Pope continued. 'Some o' them cowboys'll step up, I'm thinkin'.'

'They may not,' Jack said, 'when they see how big he is.'

Pope laughed. 'Ol' Lee won't hurt 'em much. He's a kindly sorta guy. He jus' knocks 'em down and then he lays on 'em a little bit. When they can't breathe no more, he let's 'em up. It's like bein' lain on by a buffalo, ain't at all nice. They usually give up then. Mind you, not all of 'em do. One time, in Dodge, a fella got his breath back and came at Lee again. Mind, he was half-seas over. Lee socked 'im an' he flew through the air into the crowd an' knocked 'em down like ninepins.'

'I can believe that,' Jack said.

Lee paused from slinging the rocks. 'They deducted two dollars off the purse after that. Said I broke a chair in the saloon. It weren't me that broke it, it were the fella that landed in it broke it.'

'That's the truth,' Pope said. 'It weren't Lee at all. Lee gotta put up with all kindsa disrespect in this game. Name callin' somethin' terrible. You wouldn't believe it.'

The dam gave way suddenly and water pushed from underneath it, flooding out into the dry riverbed. It gathered pace over the dust and stones, on down the canyon. Lee Yoo let out a whoop of delight. 'Done her!' he cried. He slapped Pope on the back. 'Didn't take long at all.'

'Well, thank you kindly,' Jack said. 'Made my day a lot easier.'

'That's what we aim to do,' Pope said. 'Now, you comin' to the prize fight, mister? Ol' Lee don' need supporters but he likes 'em.'

'I'll do my best,' Jack said. 'It's kinda difficult for me in town right now. To tell the truth, I ain't supposed to be there at all.'

'Kinda the same situation as ol' Lee,' Pope said. 'Always difficult for him. People always tryin' to get the better of him because he's a Chinaman an' a prize fighter. Truth is he's stronger than the whole bunch of them put together an' he's got more brains than 'em too.'

'Can't say that's the same as me,' Jack grinned.

The force of water had pushed the clay lining aside and was flooding out between the timbers now. In minutes, the flow was strong and steady. The dam would be difficult to repair.

'Want me to take her down some more?' Lee asked.

'That's OK,' Jack said. 'The water'll do the rest.'

'My turn,' Jack said. 'If you boys wants to walk a mile down the creek with me, you can s'lect any timber you like. I got an old broken-down homestead back there. Plenty of timber.'

Jack left his horse and set off back with Pope and Lee.

'Nice day for a walk down a creek,' Pope said to Lee, who peeled with laughter. 'How come you two laugh so much?' Jack said.

'Our philosophy, ain't it?' Pope said. 'If ya got a sense

of humour, darned shame not to use it.'

Lee nodded in serious agreement. 'Makes the days pass with greater enjoyment.'

'Trouble is,' Pope went on, 'most folks got a sense of humour, but they don' hardly never use it. Then there's other folks jus' ain't got no sense of humour at all. Well, ain't nothin' you can do for them.'

'Them's about fifteen per cent of people ain't got no sense of humour at all, in my estimation,' Lee added.

'Hear that?' Pope said. 'Ol' Lee ain't hardly never wrong when it comes to figures.' He lifted his hat by the crown vertically off his head with one hand and scratched the exact top of his head with the other until a clump of hair stood straight up. Jack chuckled. 'See,' Pope said, 'ain't hard to make someone laugh.'

'Sure ain't,' Jack said. 'I think you've got a grand philosophy there.'

At the mission, Lee and Pope selected a pine beam from the collapsed porch for an axle. Lee shouldered it and they walked back up the creek together. Between them, they carried the beam up the steep path and Lee carried it again, on across the plain to the wagon. The sky was wide above them. Buffalo grass waved in the breeze and apart from a few isolated clumps of grey-barked hackberry bushes, nothing stood above it for miles.

Lee held up the wagon while Jack and Pope freed the broken axle. He set it down gently. 'Ain't so bad,' Jack said. 'Ain't broke all the way through. We can nail a patch on it, bind it up with some rope. Should hold until you make town. You can keep the timber and give it to a carpenter to make a new axle with. Save buyin' another piece.'

An hour later, with the job done, Lee and Pope set off towards the town. They would have to make the long detour east, the route that Blacklake's cattle had to take, in order to find a way down off the ridge. They called out a so-long to Jack, all the time sharing some private joke. Jack could hear them laughing to each as the wagon rolled away over the high plain. Jack himself scrambled back down the zigzag to the dam, collected his horse and picked his way over the flowing stream, back down to the mission.

The moment Jack emerged from the mouth of the creek he was aware of two things. Above him, the Comanche on horseback was keeping watch and there was a horse tethered in the shade under the stand of cottonwoods. At first Jack thought Moses must have come, then he realized he didn't recognize the horse. It was a grey-and-white mare. Jack couldn't recall seeing her in the stable. As Jack walked his horse up to the homestead, a cowboy emerged from round the far side of the building. It was Clem from the Diamondback. Jack hadn't seen him since the day he took him to Adela to be patched up after his rum-in with the deputies.

'You lookin' for somethin'?' Jack said.

'They said I'd most likely find you out here,' Clem said. 'I asked in the saloon.'

'Yeah?'

Clem seemed to be building himself up to telling Jack something. Jack dismounted and led his horse over to the cottonwoods. The cowboy stood anxiously waiting for Jack to face him. The swellings on his face had gone down, leaving a yellow bruise across his nose and under his eyes.

105

'Someone took a dislike to you, too?' Clem said, trying to comment on Jack's bruises with forced cheerfulness.

'S'right,' Jack said. He finished hitching the horse to the cottonwood branch and turned to face Clem while he untied the pick and shovel from the saddle. 'You didn't come all the way out here to tell me about my good looks,' Jack said.

'Mister, there ain't no easy way to say this. So I'm just gonna say it.' Jack could hear in his voice that the news he brought was the worst. 'Mister, I gotta tell you, Moses got shot.'

'What?' Jack was stunned.

'Mister,' Clem went on miserably, 'Moses is dead. Bull Brown shot him. The deputies were there too.'

Jack's face hardened. 'How come?'

'They said he stole Miss Blacklake's horse and sold it to the Comanches. They said they found it out here somewhere.'

Jack was silent. The righteous fury, made up of grief and anger, which boiled inside him was not visible to Clem. All Clem could see was Jack's expressionless face, a mask which betrayed no emotion. Jack's blue eyes seemed to look beyond Clem, into the future, as if they were focusing on what he knew he must do.

'You gonna take 'em?' Clem asked. 'They'll be waitin' for you. Clovis Blacklake will set a trap. He's the kinda guy don't leave nothin' to chance.'

Jack was silent.

'If y'are, you're gonna need some help. There are three of them. I'll help you. Them deputies are the ones that jumped me. Bull Brown's the one had 'em do it.'

106

Jack seemed to see Clem again, as though he'd forgotten he was there for a time.

'Thanks,' he said. 'I appreciate that.'

'I got a screw of coffee in my saddle-bag,' Clem said. 'I could boil us up a cup.'

'That'd be mighty nice.' Jack sat down underneath the cottonwoods while Clem busied himself with the fire. The heat of the afternoon was beginning to die down and the sun was sinking in the sky. Jack looked over the old, broken homestead building, thinking what a fool he'd been to invest his hopes in this place. This place or any place, he thought bitterly. It seemed as if all these long years since the war ended, he'd been searching for a home. Every time he thought he'd found one, something had got in the way and he'd moved on. His trail had been a lonesome one.

Jack pushed self-pity aside. He knew what he had to do. Sure, Blacklake was behind this. Bull Brown would never act without Blacklake's say-so. And Blacklake would never let the mission go without a fight. It had been wishful thinking to pin his hopes on Adela's powers of persuasion. Blacklake wanted the whole of this part of the panhandle and everyone in it for himself. There were just a few who had it in them to stand up against him. With a little encouragement, Moses had been one. Clem was another. Because he'd suffered at the hands of the deputies, he'd changed from being just another cowhand goofing off in the saloon, to someone who was prepared to do what was right. And there was kindly Adela who did her best, but could not see her brother for the tyrant really was.

Clem brought a mug of coffee over to Jack. Jack told

107

him about the basket of food keeping cool down the well. Clem helped himself to chicken and pie. Jack didn't feel like eating. He sipped his coffee and checked his Peacemakers. They were clean, oiled and loaded. It had been a while since he had used them though, so while Clem ate Jack set up a bench on the far side of the homestead and balanced some rusty tin cans on it for target practice.

At first, Jack's aim was off. But after a few rounds he got his eye in, until many of the shots sent a can spinning up into the air.

'Nice shootin',' Clem called admiringly. 'Guess you've done that before.'

'Some,' Jack said. 'But not for a while.'

Jack kept at it for an hour or more. Clem found him more old cans and pieces of wood to shoot at. Eventually, Jack could guarantee to hit the target every time. After this, Jack got Clem to throw cans high into the air for him to shoot at before they hit the ground. He followed the same pattern. Some misses at first, then he found his aim until every shot sent a can lurching off its trajectory high overhead.

Then Clem tried. He checked the chamber of his Colt .45 and strode fifty paces back from the row of tin cans. He took a moment to focus on his targets, then fired fast from the hip. The cans spun in all directions. He never missed once. After he had emptied the chamber, he glanced modestly at Jack. 'Ain't a whole lot to do out at the Diamondback, once the work is done. The boys're always havin' shootin' competitions in the evenings.'

Jack grinned in admiration. 'I'm mighty glad you're on

my side, that's all. You're a helluva shot.'

'Thanks.'

'Anyhow, best you ride back,' Jack said. 'No point in lettin' 'em know you're helpin' me until we have to. Besides, I need some more shells. Could you pick me up a coupla boxes at the hardware store? An' I gave my Winchester to Moses; guess that might be at the stables somewhere.'

Clem agreed to get the shells and look for the rifle and to deliver them the following day. He said he would also try to find out what Blacklake had planned for Jack.

Blacklake was bound to use some of the Diamondback cowboys if he had some kind of ambush in mind. They were Clem's friends and would tell him.

10

'Won't have no more trouble from that Injun, boss.' Bull Brown dashed into Blacklake's office, without knocking, and ran up to stand in front of the huge desk. He looked mighty pleased with himself. 'Turns out he was a horse-thief.' He stood with a smug grin over his face, waiting for Blacklake's approval.

Adela stood beside her brother. They had been discussing the arrangements for her approaching eye surgery when Bull burst in. It would mean a long spell in the New York hospital and Adela's eyes would be bandaged shut for three months after the procedure. Although she was frightened at the thought of it, it was becoming almost impossible for her to live a normal life, let alone teach at the school. Her short-sightedness was becoming acute and her sense of colour was worsening. She was left with no choice. The latest communication from the hospital described an as yet untried procedure which was to be performed by an ophthalmologist newly arrived from Germany. It would cost $1,000. Her brother, as usual, had immediately offered to pay.

110

'What?' Blacklake said. 'Moses from the stable?'

'Ridiculous,' Adela snapped. Her dislike of Brown showed.

'He sold your horse, Miss Adela,' Bull went on, with a self-satisfied grin on his face. 'I recovered it myself.'

'Who to?' Adela said indignantly. 'This is nonsense.'

'Injun braves were seen riding your horse out of the stable by Silas Johnson, one of my deputies.'

'I know who Silas Johnson is. I knew him when he was a little boy. He was a cheat and a bully then and I expect he still is now.'

'And you got the horse back?' interrupted Blacklake.

'Found him tethered out by the old mission, when we brought that drifter in. Injuns must have abandoned him. See, Comanche braves only like their own ponies. They don' know what to do with a pure-bred horse like yours, Miss Adela. They probably abandoned him. Tied him up and left him to starve. Never does no good to trust an Injun in my book, not even Moses.'

'How can you say that? How can you say that about Moses?' Righteous fury boiled inside Adela. 'He was a sweet child out at the mission and has never done anything to harm anyone in his life. Anyway, you know perfectly well the Comanche love horses, they care for them just as much as they care for themselves. They would never leave one to starve.'

Bull brushed her anger aside. 'I'm just sayin' what I saw, ma'am.'

'All right, all right,' Blacklake said. 'So what's happened to Moses?'

'I went to arrest 'im,' Bull continued pompously, 'in my

official duty as sheriff. He went for a Winchester he had stashed away in the stable. Now, that weren't his Winchester. Moses never had no repeating rifle. He had a scattergun he used for huntin' rabbits and such. He must have stole the Winchester from someone. No one gonna give him a Winchester, are they?'

'So,' Blacklake insisted, 'what happened?'

'Like I said, he went for the rifle,' Bull said proudly. 'But I was too quick for 'im. I shot 'im in the back before he could turn round.'

Adela screamed and sank down into a chair.

Bull added, 'It's what you wanted, ain't it, boss?' Suddenly he realized that Blacklake's reaction was the opposite of what he had expected.

Blacklake was speechless for a moment. Then he yelled at Bull to get out. 'Find somebody to work at the stables,' he shouted. 'I ain't got time for this.'

Bull looked pale and afraid as he backed out of the room.

'When you come outa the hospital,' Blacklake tried to resume their conversation, 'you come back to the Diamondback. You'll need a good long rest. I'll take care of you.'

'How could he do that to Moses?' Adela sobbed, tears running down her face.

'He's over-zealous sometimes, is all,' Blacklake said. 'He keeps good order in the town. He's loyal. He's very fond of you.'

Adela looked at her brother, appalled. 'You still want me to go courtin' him, don't you? How could you think that? That – that – murderer!'

112

Blacklake snapped. The worry of Adela's eye operation; the strain of overseeing the round-up ready for his biggest cattle drive yet; this nonsense claim on the old mission house; the drifter stirring things up against him and now, Bull taking initiative on his own and blurting it out in front of Adela in a way that implicated him, was too much. He wanted to be in control. He had to keep Bull on a tight leash, he had to get rid of the drifter and Adela had to do what she was told.

'Bull Brown is the sheriff,' he said, his voice rising. 'He is loyal and responsible and looks out for our interests. But most important of all, there is no one better in this place. This is the panhandle. This is a cattle town full of cowpunchers and store clerks and they are all a lot younger than you are. Bull Brown will protect you. You shouldn't confuse what a man does for a living with what he is like as a husband. That is not for a woman to think about.' Blacklake was shouting now.

Adela jumped up and ran out of the room. 'You hear me out,' Blacklake yelled at her. 'When you come back from the eye hospital, you will look kindly on Nathan Brown and you will like it, missy!'

Adela rode directly to the schoolhouse, which she set about cleaning from top to bottom to take her mind off her misery. The town was packed with visitors. The saloon was full and there were tables and chairs along the boardwalk outside. Every seat was taken by men drinking, talking and playing cards. Across the street, the Johnsons had put up red, white and blue paper bunting across the front of their shop. Pa Johnson had nailed a large painted sign over the door which read 'Johnson and Sons Hardware offers congratulations to The Diamondback Ranch and welcomes all customers'. Johnson had ordered in several cases of Tennessee bourbon, which were stacked behind his shop door. He intended to sell them to Charlie at an inflated price when the saloon ran dry, which he knew it would later in the weekend. To this end he encouraged everyone who came into the shop, quite insistently, to 'go over to the saloon and wet your whistle', which Ma Johnson found faintly embarrassing.

At the end of the street, the livery stables were in chaos. Horses were packed in too tightly and no one had thought to feed or water them. They were hungry and restless. The stalls needed cleaning out and the place stank. One or two cowboys who realized that their animals were being neglected came and fed and watered them themselves and took them away, cursing the Injun who was supposed to be looking after them. Moses's body lay covered in blood-soaked straw in the stall furthest away from the door, where Bull and the deputies had made an attempt to hide it.

Bull was still hot after his encounter with Blacklake, but he was used to the cattle baron's unpredictable moods. He paced slowly up and down main street letting himself, his sheriff's badge and his Remington be seen by the incomers. His eyes were peeled for potential trouble-makers. But nothing untoward was happening.

Bull noticed Clem going into Johnson's hardware and grinned to himself at the memory of the whuppin' his deputies had given him. His finger burned with pain and the bandage, clogged with dried blood, needed changing.

114

Ordinarily, he would have gone straight to Adela to ask her to do this, but this time he was too embarrassed. To have been accidentally shot by a woman's tiny derringer, let alone Adela's, was humiliating. The pain from his finger and his confused emotions put him in a foul mood.

Bull took a walk round the town limits. There were a few tents pitched at the back of the saloon and another camp seemed to be starting beside the road out of town. But mostly people unfurled their bedrolls on the ground under the sky. The visitors were mainly young cow-punchers who had come to see the prize fight. If they were drunk enough they might put themselves up as challengers. Others were drifting from ranch to ranch, in the cowboy way, and probably had half a mind to ask for work at the Diamondback once the weekend was over. There were also a few families: thin-faced men desperately searching for somewhere to live and make a living with their tired wives and dirty, unkempt children, excited by all the people around them after their lonely journeys across the prairie. The better off had their possessions in a wagon, others had uncovered mule carts. Bull felt contempt for them all.

Numerous cooking fires had been lit. The smell of coffee and frying bacon and grits drifted across the campsites. Ragged children went from group to group offering to forage firewood for a nickel. The men lounged in front of their tents, or sat around on their bedrolls chatting and smoking.

Out at the mission, Jack set about the task of digging Moses's grave. He chose a spot behind the house, in the shade of the cottonwoods, where he had tethered Adela Blacklake's horse when Moses's Comanche brother had returned her to them. Jack guessed that this was what Moses would have wanted. When the job was done, he made a rough cross out of two branches of cottonwood, nailed and tied together.

He carved Moses's name on the crosspiece and laid it down at the head of the grave. If he couldn't bury Moses himself, he would make sure someone else did.

In town, everyone was waiting for the arrival of Lee Yoo, the prizefighter. Rumours were circulating about his size, strength and his vicious, foreign, fighting techniques. One man claimed to have met him in a bar in California and said he was so tall that when he stood up, he cracked the plaster ceiling with the top of his head. Another said that he was so heavy that a special boat had to be built for him when he sailed over from China. And then the stories of his fights got taller with each telling. He was supposed to have bitten the heads off wild animals, torn the limbs off his opponents, drunk the blood of his enemies and a grizzled, old cowhand from Colorado said he had met an Irishman who had seen him squeeze the head of a challenger until his skull cracked and his brains squirted over the ceiling. Eventually, impatience got the better of everyone. A cowboy with a reputation for being fast on horseback was dispatched to ride out of town, to see if he could see Lee Yoo and estimate how long it would be before he arrived.

11

Next morning Jack was awake at first light. At first a pink thread seemed to bleed into the inky sky along the flat horizon, then the sun gradually appeared like an orange fist out of the dark land. Daylight pushed the indigo clouds aside and the rightful colours started to soak back into the landscape. Jack climbed out of his bedroll, rekindled the dying fire and set his coffee on to brew. He lowered the bucket into the well and doused his hands and face in the pure, cold water. The shock of the icy splash woke all his senses at once, making him feel fully awake and fully alive. In an instant, everything returned to his consciousness and he knew what he had to do.

Jack fed and watered his horse, then turned to his own breakfast. He finished the remains of Adela's chicken and pie and washed it down with hot coffee. The morning air on his face was crisp and new. While he had been eating, daylight had fully returned. He walked over to the mouth of the canyon to check the progress of the stream. The water was slowly finding its old pathway, the best way down the coulee. It had 200 yards to go before it reached the mouth of the canyon and the mission. Lee Yoo had done a good job: the flow was steady and unstoppable. Jack judged the stream would be running parallel to the mission by evening.

Half an hour later Clem arrived. There were so many incomers in the town, he said, they were falling over each other like rabbits in a warren. Bull Brown was stalking the place looking for trouble. The deputies were taking it in turns helping at their parents' store and patrolling with Brown. There had almost been a fight between Pa Johnson from the store and Charlie from the saloon because Mrs. Johnson and her sons had been selling bottles of Tennessee bourbon to the incomers for less than the saloon's prices. Eventually, Johnson had agreed to sell all his remaining cases to Charlie at wholesale price to prevent Charlie banning him from the bar.

A cowboy who rode out to find the prizefighter yesterday had returned to tell everyone that he would be arriving in town this morning. The Chinaman would perform some feats of strength outside the saloon this evening and the fight would be tonight.

The cowboy had said the fighter travelled with another man who had told him that if he had arrived a few minutes earlier he would have seen the fighter eating the only food he ever ate before a fight. This was fresh snake-meat which the fighter always took raw. He had caught a rattler with his bare hands that afternoon, apparently. The fighter's companion showed the skin to the cowboy.

'You believe that?' Clem said uncertainly. 'Eating a rattler's one thing, but catching it with your bare hands, I dunno.'

118

'Blacklake expectin' me?' Jack asked.

Clem looked as if he had been dreading this question. 'Best if you just rode on out,' he said. 'He's collected up the two meanest sonsabitches from the Diamondback and made them into his private bodyguard. Their job is to keep a special lookout for you. And on top of that there's Bull Brown and the Johnson boys. They're all on the lookout. They figure the best way to keep in with Blacklake is to bring him your corpse.'

Jack seemed to take time to absorb the information. 'There's one thing I want you to do for me,' he said at last. 'I dug a grave over by the cottonwoods. It ain't likely I'll be comin' back here, so I want you to bury Moses in it. He grew up here, so it's a kinda homecoming'.'

'Sure,' Clem said quietly. 'I'll do that. But you're not going into town are you? There's no need. Maybe you can stay away for a while then come back later. In a few months, when this has all died down, you could take a job here. You're a useful guy. Blacklake would give work to a guy like you, maybe let you work out here. He's a businessman, he don't have to like the guys he gives work to. He ain't like that.'

Jack looked at Clem. 'Two kindsa people in the world,' he said matter-of-factly. 'When there's a fight comin', there's the ones who only take it on if they know they can win. An' then there's the ones who jus' fight anyway.'

Clem grinned. 'I guess I know which one you are. Blacklake thinks you might call him out at the prize fight.'

'Why? Does that bother him?'

'It's gonna be a proud moment for him, with him makin' a speech, telling the whole town how great he is.

119

He thinks you might wanta call him out in front of everybody.'

'Well then, I just might,' Jack said grimly. 'Where's he gonna make his speech?'

'In front of the saloon, just before the prize fight. He's gonna have two Diamondback boys on the roof of the saloon with Winchesters. He's gonna have the Johnsons in the hardware store an' he's gonna have Bull in the sheriff's office across the street.' Clem smiled. 'An he's gonna have me.'

Jack looked surprised. 'You?'

'Inside the saloon. For back-up. That's what he tol' me.' Clem grinned. 'Turns out Blacklake ain't so smart after all.' Then he added, 'Damn, I hate those Johnsons. If they start any shootin', it'll be me that finishes it.'

'Well,' Jack said, 'looks like we can make a plan.'

The crowd started to gather outside the saloon in the early evening. A trestle-stage had been put up in the middle of the street ready for Blacklake to make his speech. Bull Brown leaned against the doorway of the sheriff's office, picking his teeth with a matchstick and watching the crowd. On the roof of the saloon opposite there were two cowboys with Winchesters looking down on the street. Further down, on the same side as the sheriff's office, Bill and Silas Johnson stood outside the hardware store, gunbelts buckled on and deputy stars glinting in the sunlight of late afternoon.

Just as the entertainment was about to start Clem emerged from the front door of the saloon. He gave a sharp whistle to attract the attention of the men on the roof. 'You boys want me to get you a beer?'

'Damn right we do. It's hot as hell up here.'

Clem disappeared back into the saloon, passing Lee Yoo followed by Luther Pope coming out of the doorway. The crowd cheered. Everyone's attention was on the strongman. Lee struck a series of poses to show off his bulging muscles and after each pose there was a murmur of admiration from the crowd. Then he climbed down the steps to the street where there was a line of barrels waiting for him. Clovis Blacklake appeared in the saloon doorway to watch.

'These here barrels are filled with sand,' announced Pope grandly. 'Lee Yoo, who is probably the strongest man you've ever seen, is gonna raise one above his head, right here and now. This is the first of his amazing feats of strength, ladies and gentlemen, because each barrel weighs nigh on one hundred pounds deadweight.' The crowd gasped.

Lee gave a small, formal bow to the crowd and pushed the barrel over on to its side in front of him. He bent his knees, squatted down and gripped the rims of the barrel hard. He closed his eyes for a moment and breathed in sharply through his nose, every fibre of his body tense. Then, with a huge roar, he swung the barrel up above his head. Holding it up there with his arms straight as ramrods, he pushed upwards with his thighs until he was standing up again. Veins bulged in his neck, his face turned blood-red and his whole body shook with the strain. After a few moments of holding the keg aloft, letting out another great roar, he threw it down in front of him, causing the shocked front row of the crowd to jump

121

backwards. There were screams and shouts of admiration and surprise as the barrel burst open in an explosion of sand. The crowd roared with delight and a tidal wave of applause engulfed the proudly grinning Lee.

While all this was going on, Clem had slipped unnoticed out of the saloon door holding two bottles of beer. He quietly made his way round the back of the building where Blacklake's two lookouts had left their ladder. Jack was waiting for him there with a length of rope left over from the well. Clem, followed by Jack, climbed the ladder. The guards were craning over the front of the roof, wholly absorbed in watching Lee's feat of strength, their Winchesters propped beside them.

Jack and Clem were on them before they knew it. They took one of the guards each, cracked them across the backs of their heads with the handles of their pistols and tied the men back to back while they were still too stunned to resist. Clem produced two bandannas from his pocket and they gagged the men tightly. They lay them on their sides, tied their feet together and left them. As the crowd roared at the front of the building, Clem and Jack climbed down the ladder at the back. Clem made his way round to the front of the saloon again. Jack slipped down behind the row of buildings to the stables at the far end of the street.

Blacklake's men had done a good job of tending to the horses, although they were still crowded in at two or three to a stall. More were tethered out back under Moses's fig tree and at the rail out front. Jack began with the horses tethered to the fig tree. He quietly walked from one to the other, unhitching them all, patting them gently and talking to them reassuringly as he did so. He moved from stall to stall inside the stable, quietly unhitching the horses, taking care not to startle them. The animals moved slightly, but stayed obediently where they were for the moment, hardly aware that they were free.

Jack stepped out into the street and quietly pulled the stable door to. He loosened the reins of the line of horses at the rail. Then he opened the stable door wide enough for a curious animal to get out. Again, the horses at the rail remained where they were for the moment. Shouts and cheers came from the other end of the street. Lee Yoo was still wowing the crowd. Jack pulled his hat down low over his eyes, slipped round the back of the stable and made his way up behind the row of buildings. While everyone's attention was still on the strongman, keeping his head down, he made his way down a side alley and eased his way into the crowd. Clem was in the saloon doorway, Bull Brown was in front of the sheriff's office and the Johnson boys were outside the store. None of them noticed.

After more barrel-lifting from Lee and more cheers from the crowd, Pope reminded everyone that a one hundred dollar purse was the prize for anyone who could knock Lee Yoo down. A few big men from out of town consulted seriously together and looked as if they might step up, but the majority of the cowboys were suddenly silent. The fighter would welcome all challengers, Pope said. Proceedings would begin at eight o'clock on the stage inside the saloon. Now it was time for Blacklake's speech.

Blacklake stepped on to the trestle-stage and looked

over the crowd. His black jacket and hat were immaculate, his tie was evenly laced and his black boots shone. He swept the sides of his jacket back to reveal his hand-tooled gunbelt and his two silver six-shooters. His expression was extreme pride mixed with arrogance. He was an emperor addressing his subjects. 'People of the panhandle,' he began, 'cowboys from the Diamondback ranch, men and women from the town, next week the seventh cattle drive will begin from outa my ranch, the Diamondback. It will be the biggest. It will travel the furthest and it will make the most profit. It is seven years since the war ended and by hard work, starting from small beginnings, I have become the richest man I know. I built this town for you and your children to live in and I turned the empty plains into a ranch for longhorns. Seven years ago there was only buffalo and savages here, but I drove them off—'

Blacklake suddenly broke off from his speech. He seemed to be staring over the heads of the crowd at something behind them. Members of the crowd began to turn round to see what had distracted him. A group of horses was standing untethered in the middle of the street, outside the stable. More were filing out through the open stable door. Someone gave a shout and began running down the street to the stable, more people joined him until most of the crowd was running to try to catch the animals. The horses, startled by the sudden movement and the mass of people running towards them, turned tail and began to trot in the opposite direction. The closer the crowd got, the more they picked up speed until one by one they began to gallop down the road and out of town, their manes flying, glorying in their new-found freedom.

Blacklake stepped down off the trestle-stage and stared down the street in disbelief. The deputies had run down towards the stable ahead of the crowd. Bull stopped chewing his matchstick and stood gazing after them. Clem quickly crossed the street and stood beside him. The crowd melted away, until Blacklake realized that one man remained facing him. It was Jack.

Blacklake staggered backwards, letting out a yelp of surprise and nearly falling on to the stage. Bull wheeled round, hesitated for a second while he took in what was going on and went for his gun. That second was long enough for Clem to press the barrel of his Colt into the side of Bull's thick neck. Clem unhooked Bull's Remington from its holster, dropped it on the ground and kicked it away. Bull looked desperately up to the roof of the saloon, but there was no sign of the cowboys with Winchesters.

'I'm calling you out, Blacklake,' Jack shouted.

Blacklake looked around wildly for help. Clem jabbed his pistol barrel hard into Bull's neck again.

'What?' Blacklake seemed stunned.

'Your men killed my friend. You took his water and you took his land. An' I was gonna live there with him.'

'You no-good drifter,' Blacklake hissed. 'I built this town. I made this land what it is. And it all belongs to me, not you and some crippled Injun. I shoulda shot you like a sick dog first time I saw ya.' He flicked back the sides of his jacket, exposing his pearl-handled pistols in their polished holsters.

The two men looked straight into each other's eyes. Jack sensed Blacklake going for his gun and his hand instinctively whipped his Peacemaker out of its holster as he leapt to the right to avoid the shot. Right at that moment, there was a woman's shrill scream and Adela was between them, running towards him. For a second she blocked his line of sight. He heard Blacklake's gun and felt the searing, hot metal burn his side. He fired himself and saw Blacklake go down. Adela was screaming and crying. Blacklake was propped against the trestle-stage, his right hand, still holding his pistol, was clasped across his left shoulder. His face was twisted with pain. The two deputies were suddenly there, unholstering their guns. Clem shoved Bull to the ground and shot at them both. Their pistols went spinning away. Clem pointed his gun straight back at Bull. 'You kick them pistols over here or I'm gonna plug your sheriff,' he yelled.

'Do what he says,' Bull sobbed.

Adela helped Jack up. 'You're hurt,' she breathed, noticing the blood welling through the side of his shirt.

'Ain't nothin' but a scratch,' Jack said. 'You got between us. I couldn't see him.'

'Let me tend the wound. Come back to the schoolhouse.'

'No. I'm leavin'. I can't stay here now. My horse is all saddled up down at the stable.'

'Leaving? You can't, Jack. Not like this.'

'Gotta move on, Miss Adela, but I ain't sayin' goodbye.'

Blacklake called out to Adela. The blood had drained from his face and he held his gun in his lap. A horrified crowd had gathered, keeping well back.

'You went to him,' he croaked. 'You went straight to him, not to me. He coulda killed me, Adela. I got a bullet in my arm right now.'

Adela approached her brother. 'I'll take care of it, Clovis, don't you worry now.'

Jack turned away and started to walk with slow, hesitant steps towards the stables. Bull saw his chance and dived for his gun. He snatched it up and a shot rang out. Jack half-turned, surprised, and saw Adela's face looking at him.

Bull slumped heavily to the ground. Blacklake held his silver pistol unsteadily in his hand. 'You're a damn fool, Bull Brown. You've always been a damn fool. You don't know when to begin and when to end.'

Silas and Bill, the deputies, glanced at each other and sidled back through the crowd to the store. Clem collected up their pistols and Bull's Remington. A couple of men from the crowd helped Blacklake to his feet. 'Like me to get you a whiskey from the saloon, Mr Blacklake?' one of them said.

'No,' Blacklake said sharply. 'Just help me over to the schoolhouse.'

At the western end of the street, outside the stables, Jack sat on his bay. His mule, alongside him, was loaded with all his possessions. The sunset was blood-red and gold across the sky behind him. Great furrows of cloud reflected the majestic light of the dying day. It was hard to tell from this distance, but he seemed to be leaning slightly to one side in the saddle. He raised his arm in a goodbye salute. Clem waved back and called out, but Jack was too far away to hear. Luther Pope and Lee Yoo watched him from the porch of the saloon. Adela myopically peered down the street but could not see far enough. With a final wave, Jack

127

turned his horse and headed out towards the flaming sun which seemed to be resting for a moment on the dark shelf of the horizon.

Lee Yoo stepped down off the saloon porch, scooped up Blacklake and carried him towards the schoolhouse. Blacklake grimaced at the pain in his arm.

Adela turned to Clem, who had been staring after Jack. 'You'll come with us, won't you? I might not be able to manage on my own.'

A man in a dark jacket appeared out of the crowd, produced a tape measure from his pocket and ran it matter-of-factly along the length of Bull Brown's corpse. His assistant brought up a horse-drawn cart and took old Bull away. Luther Pope set up a chalkboard outside the saloon door with the message '$100 Purse. 9 o'clock.' Underneath, Charlie had written 'Tennessee Whiskey. New Delivery'.

12

As soon as they heard shooting and saw a crowd of people running down the street towards the livery stable, Ma and Pa Johnson ducked back inside the store. They pulled the blinds, turned the 'Open' sign to 'Closed' and locked the door. They had not seen what had happened, but the sound of gunfire was enough to make them afraid. They cowered behind the counter, unsure of what to do to protect their stock.

Moments later someone shook the door violently from outside and shouted to be let in. It was Silas. Bill was right behind him. Pa Johnson unlocked the door and the two deputies tumbled in like unruly schoolboys. They gabbled an unbelievable story about a gunfight in which a drifter and Mr Blacklake had shot each other and then Blacklake had shot Bull Brown.

'Musta bin a mistake,' Pa Johnson reflected.

'No. It weren't no mistake,' Silas said nervously. 'He shot him square on.'

'Well, what about this drifter?'

'Rode off.' Bill chipped in. 'Jus' walked on down to the

129

stable, took his horse an' rode off. He was wounded though. Took a bullet in the side.'

'Well, whatcha gonna do about it? You're the town deputies. Ain't ya gonna go after him?'

'Dunno, Pa,' Silas said. His face was pale and he looked genuinely frightened. 'Mr Blacklake shot ol' Bull an' seeing as we're Bull's deputies, maybe we'd better jus' lay low for a while.'

'That's right,' Ma Johnson agreed. 'You keep outa the way if there's any shootin'. I don't want my boys gettin' hurt an' that's a fact.'

'Shaddup, Ma,' Pa Johnson snapped. 'This is the boys' chance to make sheriff.' He was becoming excited as thoughts of status for his family rose in his brain. 'Or one of 'em can. Ol' Bull Brown's gone. Town ain't got no sheriff. Mr Blacklake'll probably make you sheriff, Silas, seeing as how you're older. Might even make you both sheriff. Damn, that'd be a proud day for me an' Ma.'

Silas was shaking. 'You don' get it, Pa. This drifter, he's a killer. He called Mr Blacklake out, right in front of everybody. Me an' Bill, we may be deputies but we ain't no gunslingers.'

Pa became angry. 'Now, you listen to me, Silas, an' you, Bill, an' you listen good while I explain to you.' His voice was cold and hard as steel. It was the voice which had made his sons afraid of him when they were boys. It still did now. 'You bring in this drifter or you shoot him. That way you'll have dealt with the man who shot Mr Blacklake. Mr Blacklake's a rich an' powerful man. He'll make you sheriff an' give you a reward too, mos' likely. Anyways, I thought you said this drifter'd been shot. Can't two of you deal with a man who's already carryin' a slug?' He paused, glaring at his sons, just as he had always done. 'Now, you jus' get out that door an' you fin' this drifter. An' when you find him you either take him to Mr Blacklake or you shoot him dead. An' don' you come back till you've done it.'

Pa unlocked the shop door and his sons stepped outside without looking back at him.

It was getting dark. There was chaos outside the stable, as people were still trying to round up their horses and get them back inside. At the other end of the street, groups of cowboys were heading for the saloon and crowds stood around exchanging different versions of what had happened earlier. Groups of men from out of town studied the signboard outside the saloon advertising the hundred dollar prize.

Silas and Bill skulked along the side of the buildings, trying to remain unnoticed.

'This is what we'll do,' Silas said. 'We'll look for the drifter, but we ain't gonna look too hard. An' we sure as hell ain't gonna find him.'

'I ain't takin' on no gunslinger,' Bill agreed.

'In the mornin' we'll follow his trail out of town. He'll either have bled to death by then or he'll be too weak to fight. Either way we'll put a coupla slugs in him jus' to make sure.'

'What're we gonna tell Pa?' Bill asked nervously.

'We ain't gonna tell him nothin'. We're gonna fin' Mr Blacklake an' let him know we've bin lookin' for the drifter, but we can't carry on now on accounta it's dark. We'll find him in the morning. That'll make us look good.' Silas gave a weasel grin. 'He might even make me sheriff right away.'

In Adela's parlour behind the schoolroom Clovis
Blacklake lay back on the chaise longue. His face, covered
with a film of sweat, was as yellow as parchment in the light
of the oil lamp. His cheeks were smudged black where
perspiration had caused dye from his moustache to run.
His thin lips were tight with pain. Adela busied herself
closing the drapes and looking out bandages, scissors and
ointments. Lee Yoo and Clem stood awkwardly by.

'You stay, Clem,' Blacklake said through clenched
teeth. 'Tell the Chinaman to go. The prize fight must go
ahead.' Lee understood perfectly of course, and turned to
leave.

'I'm going to have to cut the sleeve of this jacket,' Adela
said.

'No, no,' Blacklake protested. He grimaced as he eased
his injured arm out of the sleeve, brusquely waving away
Adela's help. 'I almost shot you,' he said. 'Why did you run
in between us like that? You heard him call me.'

'Jack is a good man, Clovis,' Adela said quietly.
'Whatever has been said or done.'

'I can't believe I almost shot you. My own, dear sister.'
Blacklake's face was sunken in. The horror at what might
have happened seemed to concern him more than the
pain of his wound.

The dark material of the jacket was wet with blood and
the shirtsleeve underneath was soaked red. Adela quickly
and gently washed the blood from his arm, dipping a
clean cotton rag into a bowl of warm water. With the blood
cleaned away, a red slash, like a knife-wound, was clearly

visible, scored across the side of the man's bicep. It was a flesh wound. The bullet had not penetrated the arm.

'I'll bandage it,' Adela said. 'You've been lucky, Clovis. You stay there and rest awhile. Clem and I will get anything you want.'

'I have to get down to the saloon to see the fight,' Blacklake said.

'That won't start for another hour,' Clem told him. 'I'll get them to delay it to give you a chance to rest up.'

There was a cautious knock at the door. When Adela opened it, Silas and Bill Johnson stood there, anxiously turning their hats in their hands.

'Schoolroom door was open, so we came on through. . . .' Silas hesitated. 'We kinda wanted to see how Mr Blacklake was doin'. Folks in the town is anxious to know.'

Adela was surprised to see them. 'Well, you'd better come on in and see for yourselves.'

The Johnsons edged nervously into the room. Bill stared at the floor, too embarrassed to look anyone in the eye. Standing in the intimacy of Adela Blacklake's parlour, with his boss lying stretched out on the chaise longue, and Clem, of all people, standing there, Silas realized that coming here had not been a good idea.

'Folks is wonderin' how y'are, Mr Blacklake,' he began.

Blacklake eyed him with contempt. 'The hell with folks wonderin'. Where were you two no-good sonsabitches when the shootin' started? You're supposed to be town deputies.'

Adela flinched at her brother's language.

'Sir, we was—'

'I know where you were,' Blacklake thundered. 'Chasin' after horses, instead of doin' your job.'

Silas plucked up courage. 'Sir, we jus' wanted to tell you we've bin looking for the drifter. But it's dark now and we'll follow his trail in the mornin'. Bein' as how there's no sheriff now, we took on the responsibility ourselves. Well, it was me mainly took it on.' Silas attempted to sound businesslike, instead of as frightened as he was.

Clem said, 'These are the two jumped me outside the saloon.'

'We was actin' on orders,' Silas whined. 'Ol' Bull, rest 'is soul, said we hadta. It was sheriff's business on accounta you creatin' a disturbance an' breakin' the law. It weren't nothin' personal.'

Blacklake considered. 'Bull said jump and you jumped. That sure is followin' orders.'

'I didn't break no law,' Silas said. 'An' you know it. When Bull got the laugh, he jes' couldn't take it. We used to rag 'im a little, that's all.'

'I know why you've come here,' Blacklake announced suddenly. 'You want to step into Bull's boots an' me to make you sheriff.'

Silas started to protest.

'Well damnit, y'aint no good at bein' deputies, that's fer sure. Ya knock the dust outa Clem here for no good reason, ya ain't there at the gunfight an' ya can't find the drifter. You miserable paira jackasses. You get back to the saloon this evenin' an' make sure there ain't no fightin'. Then tomorrow mornin' you hand in your tin stars and get back to your hardware store. I'm realizin' I've bin surroundin' myself with the wrong people. Now skedaddle.'

Cowering against Blacklake's tongue-lashing, the Johnsons sidled out of the parlour. As they crossed the empty schoolroom, Bill's words echoed. 'What are we gonna tell Pa, Silas?'

Despite Adela's protests that he should rest longer, Blacklake began to pull on his jacket. 'Bull Brown was a good man in the early days,' he said. 'Tough as old saddle leather, but you could count on him. An' he was a fighter. Later on, after I made 'im sheriff, he got mean. Kinda wanted folks to respect 'im when he didn't give them no reason to. Then it rattled 'im when they didn't. Kept order in the town, but he did it through meanness. Those Johnson boys fitted right in there.' Blacklake walked towards the door, then he remembered and recrossed the room to kiss Adela lightly on the cheek. She was surprised by this unexpected show of affection and became flustered in front of Clem.

'I kin see there's gotta be some changes round here,' Blacklake said and headed off for the saloon with Clem behind him, leaving Adela to wonder what he had meant.

By the time Jack got to the mission, it was long after sunset. A glittering blanket of stars spread across the cloudless night sky and a silver moon lit the plains. Jack walked his horse slowly. Each footstep jarred the wound in his side and each stab of pain seemed worse than the one before. Blood was soaking his shirt. The wound was beginning to make him feverish and dizzy. His temperature was soaring and he felt burning hot, even in the cool night air.

He was relieved to make out the outline of the mission buildings and the cottonwoods. He had intended to ride south off the panhandle and into Texas after he had called Blacklake out. He hadn't reckoned on being shot. He knew he couldn't ride far and this was the only place he could rest up. This derelict house, a few old cottonwoods and the well was the nearest thing he had to a home. He clicked his tongue for the horse to stop just beside the well.

Jack lowered himself down the side of his horse, clinging on to the saddle. The animal stood calm and patient, sensing his master's pain. Jack found the bucket and holding on to the rope, kicked it over the edge of the well. He managed to smile to himself when he heard the splash and, still clinging to the saddle with one hand, hauled the bucket up with the other. He knelt down and pulled the bucket the last couple of feet and set it down on the lip of the well. He cupped his hands and scooped the sweet, pure water into his mouth. He splashed his face. The water danced like mercury in the moonlight.

He pulled himself up by the saddle again. He was so weak now with loss of blood that every movement cost him colossal effort. His vision blurred and the fiery pain from the wound threatened to engulf him. He was unable to stand upright. Jaws of pain were gnawing at him, pulling him down.

Stooped over, he grabbed his bedroll from its leather ties at the back of his saddle and threw it over towards the nearest cottonwood. He picked up the bucket and staggered over to where his bedroll had fallen. He put the bucket down and lowered himself on to the ground beside it. Vicious thirst scorched his throat. A lonely coyote howled somewhere out in the blackness, and in the silver moonlight Jack caught sight of Moses's empty grave. He slumped backwards and, resting his head awkwardly against the trunk of the cottonwood, fell into a feverish, dream-filled sleep.

Jack sensed people stooping over him in the night. He saw Blacklake in his dreams, with the look of surprise on his face that Jack had seen on him when he first emerged from the crowd; Adela was there in the schoolroom with Moses, with golden sunlight pouring in through the windows, and everywhere he turned the Comanche, Moses's brother, was watching him. Sometimes he was close, sitting beside him like a doctor, sometimes he was far away looking down on him from a high ridge.

Pain woke Jack before dawn. Just as he had burned with fever the previous evening, now his body shook with cold. His bones had turned to ice and his flesh was frost. He tried to cover himself with the bedroll, but was shaking so much he could hardly grasp it. He tried to will the spasms to stop with some success. This gave him something to focus his mind on while he waited for daylight.

13

'Come on now, place your bets. Two to one no one can stay upright for more'n three minutes 'fore the Chinaman knocks him down.' Luther Pope had positioned himself at the saloon door to catch the cowboys before they got to the bar. He sat at a table stashing the money in a black cashbox and writing down the names of the gamblers and the sums they had wagered in a black notebook. Lee Yoo stood beside him, grinning amiably. A long line of men waiting to hand over their money snaked out of the saloon and into the street. Hardly anyone entered the saloon without placing a bet.

A list of six names had been written on the chalkboard on the bar. These were the contenders. Pope had announced that straws would be drawn to decide the order in which they would face Lee. Charlie rushed up and down the bar from customer to customer. Everyone was good-humoured and even the men waiting at the bar were patient. The room was alive with anticipation. A talking point was the pair of leather mittens which hung on display on a nail behind the bar. These were the gloves the contenders would use. Beside them hung a second pair which belonged to Lee Yoo. These looked older and more worn than the contender's pair and the leather was scuffed and cracked.

The men who had signed up to fight were surrounded by groups of friends secretively giving them advice and pressing glasses of Tennessee sheep-dip into their hands. Every now and then one of them would glance over his shoulder at Lee Yoo, sizing him up. Everyone had a theory on how to beat the Chinaman.

Eventually, Clovis Blacklake pushed his way through the crowd and climbed on to the stage. He waved for silence.

'This is the moment we've bin waiting for,' he announced grandly. 'I've put up a one hundred dollar purse for anyone who can knock down the Chinaman. I need hardly remind you that this here shindig is put on by me to celebrate seven years of cattle drives outa my ranch, the Diamondback.' Someone at the back of the room called: 'Stop the talkin' and start the fightin'.' Blacklake ignored this and went on, 'Charlie, pass me over them gloves so's I kin inspect 'em. Jus' to make sure there ain't no lead weights or nothin' in this here Chinaman's pair.' Boos from the crowd. The gloves were duly passed across the room to Blacklake, who made a great show of inspecting Lee's pair. The crowd parted and Lee climbed up on to the stage. More booing. Blacklake handed over the gloves.

Next, Luther Pope joined them on the stage and held up six straws in his hand. 'Shortest straw fights first,' he called. 'Contenders come on up.' The six burly, anxious-looking men took their straws. The shortest was drawn by

Billy Louden, who was the cook out at the Diamondback ranch. He was popular and well-known in the town. He held up his straw to loud cheers. He was an immensely strong, slow-moving man. When he took off his shirt, revealing his huge meaty arms and vast belly, the crowd cheered again. He waved to the room, enjoying the glory of the moment. Blacklake and Pope stepped down off the stage. 'I got a pocket watch an' I'll call out if he makes it to three minutes.' The crowd called encouragement. 'Get 'im, Billy,' 'Knock 'im down,' 'You kin do it, Billy.' Lee Yoo grinned away throughout all this, but his eyes rested on Pope for a moment, who stood at the foot of the stage.

Pope called 'Time started' and the two big men began to circle round, just out of each other's reach. Billy made a few lunges and swung a wild punch, but each time Lee saw it coming and ducked backwards. It was clear that while Billy was strong, Lee was too quick for him. The crowd called out encouragement and advice. 'Knock his head off, Billy,' 'Get in close and give it to him.' Billy flailed and Lee dodged. Pope called, 'One minute gone,' and held up his stopwatch. This seemed to act as a signal to Lee; he stepped back out of the range of one of Billy's lunges and as the big man lurched forward, he swung a wide arcing punch at the side of Billy's head. The thwack of the leather-gloved fist hammering into Billy's skull could be heard right across the crowded room. Billy looked confused for a moment and Lee swung a huge punch with his other fist, bang into the other side of his head. Billy staggered and seemed to have forgotten for a moment what he was supposed to be doing. His eyes lost focus. His guard wavered. Lee swung a mighty uppercut

140

which caught Billy on the tip of his chin. His legs buckled and he dropped with a thunderous crash on to the stage. The crowd howled. 'Two minutes,' yelled Luther Pope.

Two cowboys from the Diamondback helped Billy off the stage to cheers and boos from the audience. Lee Yoo, grinning again, surveyed the crowd. 'Let the Chinaman fight one-handed,' someone shouted. 'Tie one of his arms behind his back. That'd be a fair fight.' A cowboy from out of town climbed on to the stage and laced up the gloves. He launched himself at Lee before Pope called for them to start and landed a massive punch on Lee's eye. He was a lighter, quicker challenger than Billy and had clearly had some fighting experience. He skipped round Lee jabbing punches at him and caught him a cracking blow on the back of the neck, which made him stagger forward. Both men landed a few punches successfully and both were light enough on their feet to keep out of most of the trouble. When Pope shouted two minutes, it looked as if the cowboy would remain on his feet past the three minute call and win some of the gambling money, even if he didn't manage to knock Lee down. But again, Lee seemed to find another reserve of strength. He stooped low and jabbed the cowboy in the belly, cutting off his wind. The man turned away, desperately gasping for air. It looked for a moment as if he was going to give up, but then he swung a half-hearted punch and Lee went for his stomach again. The man doubled over and crumpled on to the stage.

The other fighters went the same way. Two of them managed to land strong punches, but no one was able to knock Lee down. Lee's eye was purple and badly swollen by the end of the evening. The respect the crowd gave Lee was grudging. They had all been hoping for a local man to win the purse. Blacklake presented the hundred dollars in a leather purse to Lee after the last fighter had been helped down off the stage. There was some sporadic applause. Blacklake announced that he had put fifty dollars on the bar and Charlie had been instructed that it was for one drink per man only. Cheering wildly, the whole room surged towards the bar.

Lee and Pope, who always left a saloon quickly when they had money on them, started for the exit. There was a wild yell and, from out of nowhere, a cowboy, blazing drunk, launched himself at Lee. He swung a bottle and caught Lee across the back of the head. The bottle shattered, but a good deal of the force of the blow was absorbed by Lee's pigtail. Lee turned towards him just as the man was drawing back his arm to swing a punch. Lee ducked the punch and kicked the man's legs away from under him. He collapsed backwards on to the floor. Lee threw himself down on top of him so that his belly covered the man's head. The cowboy's arms flailed wildly, his feet drummed the floor and from his muffled cries it was obvious Lee had cut off his air supply. When the cowboy's frantic movements relaxed, Lee picked himself up. Blacklake was standing there with his gun pointing at the gasping cowboy. He waved to the Johnsons, who had been drinking at the bar, and ordered them to cart the cowboy over to the jailhouse and lock him up.

While the men pressed round the bar, Lee and Luther Pope slipped out of the saloon to their wagon. Pope had arranged for a new axle to be fitted at the lumber yard the following morning. They would both rest up the next day and try to win some money at cards in the evening. The day after that they would head south-west to Fort Worth.

Blacklake sat at a table by himself at the back of the saloon, nursing a glass of Tennessee bourbon. As cowboys passed by, they thanked him and raised their glasses. He nodded to them briefly. He enjoyed the gratitude and respect of the men. The fights had provided great entertainment for money he could well afford and had made him popular. This seventh cattle drive was ushering in a new era, he thought. People had come to his town from miles around. The town was attracting investment, the ranch was firmly established and he was the richest man in the cattle business for miles. People had even started to call him a 'cattle baron', a term which he was flattered by and thought was thoroughly appropriate.

Even though they had a long history together and Bull had had his uses, Blacklake was glad to be rid of Bull Brown. Bull had become arrogant and selfish and it was clear to him now that Adela loathed him. His choice of the Johnsons as deputies said a lot about him, Blacklake thought. They were cruel, weak men and they were incompetent. Bull had obviously chosen them because they would never question his bullying ways.

He had spent too much time concentrating on running his ranch, Blacklake thought; he had left the town in Bull's hands for too long. This was a growing town where business could take root and flourish and money could be made. Bull and the Johnsons would hold the place back. It would remain a two-bit cowtown if left to them. He

143

needed somebody with strength and intelligence, somebody who could share his vision of prosperity in the future. Apart from the few storekeepers, all the other men were hired cowboys. Most of them drifted from ranch to ranch, taking orders and collecting their pay. He often admired their skill as cattle hands, but that's all they were. There was only one person, apart from his sister, who had had the courage to stand up to him recently, he reflected, and who wanted to make something of his life here. It was that drifter, the one who had called him out.

14

Dawn came up like a blood-red tear in the sky. Jack was hallucinating in and out of consciousness so much that he didn't know if he was awake or asleep. He was sometimes aware of chanting, human voices in a kind of chorus echoing through his mind. Pain took on a different dimension. He was outside himself looking down at his own agony as if it were a picture. There was an unfamiliar, bitter taste in his mouth. Above all, he craved water but had no idea how to get it. Then there was the stabbing and the talking in some strange tongue, and a man with a knife that he had heated over a fire. He remembered the knife stabbing into his side, terrifying pain as his flesh was gouged, his arms and legs being held. He remembered biting on something hard which tasted like wood. And then he remembered nothing at all.

And now he was awake and the dawn was coming up. And he was alive.

A packet of leaves was tied over his wound with leather laces that stretched around his body. He had a vile, bitter taste in his mouth, the taste of treebark and earth. A wisp of smoke curled up from the embers of a dying fire beside him. The wound in his side throbbed, but if he lay still the pain eased. There were dark, aching bruises on his wrists, as if they had been crushed under some great weight. His ankles, too, throbbed as if they were almost broken.

Jack felt too weak to move, but he could see and think clearly again. The raging fever with its dancing shapes and shadows had left him. There was a baked-clay cup beside him. He summoned all his strength to reach over for it and was barely able to lift it to his lips. He sipped, and to his surprise tasted the bitter-sweet elixir of a Comanche healing potion, greasewood, yarrow leaves, chamomile and honey. He carefully put the cup down again and lay back. Even this slight effort had lit flames of pain in his side.

Dozing in the warm morning air was pleasant enough, provided he kept perfectly still. Thirst burned in his throat. He woke again, some time later. The day was heating up. The well-bucket was beside him. He drank off the honey medicine in the cup and dipped it in. The cool, pure water was like stars and night air in his throat.

He fell in and out of sleep. Each time he woke he seemed to feel stronger and was able to notice what was around him. In the afternoon he pushed himself up on one elbow and looked about him. Someone had tethered the horse and mule to one of the cottonwoods. He realized his head was resting on his saddle. The pack had been taken off the mule and lay on the ground. The cup and the well-bucket were still beside him, but there was also something he hadn't noticed before. On the ground beside the cup was a lead bullet.

To the south, dust was being kicked up by a rider heading in this direction. He was still a long way off and moving slowly. Someone was coming out from the town. Jack felt around for his Peacemakers. They were underneath his saddle. He hauled one of the guns out of its holster, checked the chamber and let the pistol rest on his thigh. As the cloud of dust got nearer, Jack saw that it was someone driving an open wagon. After a few more minutes, Jack recognized Clem.

Leaping down off the wagon, Clem called out to Jack. He had spent the past two days looking for him on the trail south, he said. He had no idea Jack would come back to the mission.

'Two days?' Jack said. 'How long have I been here?'

'Almost three days,' Clem said. 'I shoulda knowed you'd come back here.'

'Got shot real bad,' Jack said. 'I hadda rest up somewhere.'

'What's that?' Clem said, noticing the pouch of herbs tied over Jack's wound.

'Comanche did it,' Jack said. 'They saved me.' He pushed the bullet over for Clem to see. 'They dug it outa me. Left me medicine to drink, put this poultice on me. I don't recall too much about it. They musta gave me somethin' mighty powerful, what with that an' the fever, I didn't know if I was awake or asleep or dreamin' or what.'

'He the one that did it?' Clem said, nodding in the direction of the ridge. Noconah was there on his horse.

'Guess he was,' Jack said. 'That's Moses's brother. I'm a lucky son-of-a-gun.'

'It ain't luck,' Clem said matter-of-factly. 'If you'd

147

helped my brother like you helped Moses, I'd have dug six slugs outa you.' He paused and spoke softly. 'Speakin' of Moses, that's why I came out here.' He stood up. 'Best get on with it.'

'Say some words,' Jack said.

'I ain't much good at that, but I'll try.'

Clem led the horse and wagon over to the open grave. Moses's body had been sewn into a sheet and was resting on a bed of hay in the back of the cart. When Clem had finished the burial, he put down the shovel and stood silently by the grave with his hat in his hands. He closed his eyes and spoke a prayer he remembered from childhood. When he opened them again, he looked up and saw the lone Comanche on the ridge watching over them.

'Gotta get you back to town,' Clem said. 'You've had enough lyin' out here waitin' for the Comanche to take care of you. Gotta get you back to Miss Adela's. Here,' Clem slipped the bullet into the pocket of Jack's shirt, 'Souvenir for ya.'

Clem helped Jack up and lifted him into the wagon. The effort made Jack catch his breath in pain. His wound started to bleed again. Clem sat on the tailboard for a moment to let Jack settle back in the straw.

'Blacklake sent me out lookin' for you,' Clem said.

'Yeah?' Jack said. 'To finish me off?'

Clem grinned. 'Jus' said he wanted to talk to you. Didn't say what it was about.'

'He hurt bad?' Jack asked.

'Nope. You only winged him. He went to the prize fight. Boy, you missed somethin' there. You shoulda seen the Chinaman knock six bells outa them cowboys. None of

148

'em even got close to knocking him down. Him an' his partner, they've left town now. Sure hope Blacklake puts on another prize fight.'

'When's the cattle-drive leavin?' Jack said, still unused to the fact that he had missed the last three days.

'Left yesterday,' Clem said.

'I musta been out of it. I never heard it come through.'

'Never came through here,' Clem said. 'Blacklake changed his mind. Said he wanted to conserve the mission after all. They went the long way round. Trail hands was sore as hell about that.'

'Why aren't you with them?'

'Blacklake changed his mind about that too. Said he wanted me to be manager of the Diamondback. Didn't want me away on no cattle drive. Gave me a raise too. Said he wanted me to take care of the day-to-day runnin', so he could concentrate on other interests. Whatever that means.'

'He sure is changin' his mind a lot,' Jack observed.

'Yeah. An' he says he wants me to tell him soon as I find you.'

Clem tied Jack's horse and mule to the tailboard of the wagon and they set off towards town. In spite of Clem's slow and careful driving and the generous mattress of straw, the journey was agony for Jack. Each bump and rut the old wooden wheels passed over jolted Jack's side with pain. Clem took Jack straight to Adela's.

Lying on the bed in the room at the back of the schoolhouse, Jack watched Adela gently remove the poultice from the wound. She peered closely at the gash in his side.

'Well, those Indians did as good a job as any doctor could have done,' she said. 'That wound's as clean as clean. I'll bandage it up and then you'll just have to rest.'

Jack smiled at her. 'Thanks, I appreciate that.'

'You're lucky to be alive,' she said softly. 'I never thought I'd be nursing someone who'd been shot by my own brother. You probably blame me for getting in the way, but I'm glad I did or you two might have killed each other.'

'I don't blame you,' Jack said.

'You know, I think Clovis knows he's done wrong,' Adela said. 'It's hard for a man like Clovis to admit that. But he never meant to have Moses killed, I'm sure of it. I know he's had to be tough. I know he can be ruthless. But he's a cattleman. He just wants the Diamondback to be the biggest and the best. But he's no killer. That was Bull Brown's doing.'

Jack considered what Adela had been saying. 'He shoulda reined Bull in. Bull would have done what he said.'

'I think he knows that.'

Adela brought Jack a bowl of chicken broth, plumped up his pillows and waited with him while he ate.

'That's real good,' he said, after scraping the bowl clean. With the wholesome food inside him, Jack could feel strength soaking back into his muscles. Adela closed the drapes and left Jack to sleep.

This time he dreamed of how the mission house must have been when the pastor and his wife were living there, even though he hadn't seen it then. The roof was neatly shingled, the cabin walls were true and there was a garden with blue flowers out front. The stream ran close by. The place was bathed in sunshine and the silver leaves of the cottonwoods shimmered in the warm breeze. In his dream, Moses was there, digging the well. Jack lowered the bucket to him and brought it up brimming with pure water. He felt happy and at home in a way he couldn't remember feeling before. When Jack woke, it was evening.

Adela insisted that Jack stay in bed for a few days to give the wound time to heal. At intervals she brought him bowls of corn chowder and home-baked bread. She washed and pressed his clothes and left them neatly folded in a pile on his bedside chair. In the afternoons, when school was over, she sat with him and they talked about their childhoods. She told him how she and her brother had arrived on the panhandle in a covered wagon after the death of their parents, four years before the war. That was when Blacklake staked the first land claims of what later grew into the Diamondback ranch.

Jack described growing up on the farm in Missouri and learning horse-breaking and carpentry from his father. He told her how different the land was there and how pecans and walnuts flourished, but their plum and apricot trees were all killed off by the winter frosts. In the evenings, Adela rode out to sleep at the Diamondback. She returned every morning in time to make Jack breakfast before school.

On the fourth day, early in the morning, Jack got up and dressed himself. He was still weak and had to be careful not to turn quickly in order not to tear the wound in his side. He lit the stove in the kitchen and put coffee on to percolate. He moved a chair outside the schoolhouse door so he could sit in the cool morning air while he waited for Adela. After a while, he saw Adela's buggy making its way up the street in the pale morning sunlight. She was not driving herself today as there was someone else with her. As they approached, Jack realized it was Blacklake.

Jack hurried through the schoolroom to the bedroom out back to collect his gun. He remembered Clem saying that Blacklake wanted to talk to him, but there was no sense in leaving anything to chance. He checked the chamber of his Peacemaker, buckled on his gunbelt, and went outside again. As Blacklake stepped down from the buggy, Jack saw that he wasn't wearing a gun.

'You're not supposed to be up,' Adela called brightly. 'I've brought some bacon for breakfast.'

Blacklake nodded to him curtly. The two men followed Adela into the kitchen. They sat at the table while Adela busied herself getting out the breakfast plates. There was an awkward silence between them. When Adela went outside to the yard to see if the chickens had laid any eggs overnight, Blacklake began: 'Look, there ain't no better way of sayin' this, but I wanna tell ya I regret what happened. I've bin thinkin' a lot over the past few days. Clem tol' me you were here, but I didn't wanna come before I knew what I was gonna say.'

Jack waited for him to go on. It seemed he was struggling to get his words out, as if he was unused to speaking about himself. He looked round the room, nervously avoiding Jack's eye.

'What I'm sayin' is,' Blacklake went on, 'Adela's gotta start out for the eye clinic next week. She'll go by wagon

152

up to Dodge, then take the Wells Fargo stage to Kansas City and St Louis. I can't let her go alone. I'll stay in New York while she has the surgery. I'll make sure she's settled into a convalescent home. Then I'll come back. All in all, looks like I'll be gone for a month.'

Adela came back through the kitchen door. 'Seven eggs, still warm,' she said proudly, holding them out for the men to see. She unhooked the frying pan from its place beside the small collection of cooking pots on the wall. 'Well?' she said, addressing Blacklake. 'Have you asked him?'

Blacklake looked embarrassed. 'I was on the point of it,' he said.

'You men,' Adela said lightly. 'You're all very fine at great deeds, running cattle or shooting guns. But when it comes to looking someone in the eye and saying what's on your mind, it takes a woman to do that.'

'All right, all right,' Blacklake said. He looked directly at Jack. 'I need someone to look after the town while I'm away. Clem'll take care of the Diamondback. Town ain't got no sheriff an' I've fired them two punk deputies.' Blacklake paused. 'I know you an' me, we've had great differences. You called me out an' I know why you did. But I never ordered no one to kill Moses. That was Bull that did that.'

'He did it for you,' Jack said. 'And you dammed the creek so's he couldn't live out at the mission.'

Adela turned accusingly to her brother. 'You told me the creek had dried up.'

'I know, I know. I gave Moses the job at the stables. Driving the cattle up that creek woulda saved me fifteen miles on the journey. That's a good day's drive. You don't know how much a day costs with that many head. It was just business, that's all. You wanna make money, it's a mighty tough business. You gotta be tough. I couldn't let one old homestead stand in the way of it. I offered more'n its worth to that fool pastor years ago. I offered to build him a church in town where he could do some good. But he wouldn't have none of it.'

Blacklake paused again. The smell of percolating coffee mixed with frying bacon filled the room. Adela tended to the cooking.

'Thing of it is, I founded this town. I built it up. There wouldn't be no one here at all if it wasn't for me. I want this place to thrive. I don' want it to stay no two-bit cowtown. I want it to grow. This is a land of plenty, if you act right. I bin spendin' too much time on ranch business an' not enough on thinkin' about the town. With ol' Bull in charge this was an ol' fashioned cowboy town run by ol' fashioned cowboy ways. Drinkin', fightin' an' shootin' and never givin' a damn about tomorrow.

'When I'm in New York I'm gonna see some bankers, see if we can't get some big-time investment down here. You could build a railhead here. Think what that would mean. No more cattle-drives, people comin' to work here. The railway stretches east coast to west coast now. Why can't we have a line runs north to south? It could run down from Kansas City through the panhandle. In a few years the territories will all be opened up. They'll need a railway then. I bin building for the future ever since we got here an' I ain't stoppin' now.'

Adela screamed. She had been so entranced with her

brother's words, that she hadn't noticed the bacon begin to burn. She grabbed a cloth and wrapped it round the iron handle of the pan and lifted it off the stove. She flipped the rashers on to three plates with a fork and cracked the eggs into the pan.

'This town,' Blacklake continued, 'needs runnin' in the right way.' There was a new seriousness in his voice and he looked Jack directly in the eye. 'It needs someone strong an' fair-minded. Man like that is hard to find. I've bin thinkin' I'd make you an offer. I'll let you have the old mission property if you'll take on the job of sheriff an' take care o' the town while I'm away. There ain't no one else here who can do it. When I get back from New York, if you still want it, I'll get deeds drawn up so the mission house is yours, all legal and proper. It kinda goes with the job.'

'That mission house belonged to Moses,' Jack said. 'It ain't yours to give away.'

Blacklake smiled. 'That's why I'm askin you,' he said. 'I want someone strong and fair-minded. Trouble with those deeds is, they ain't nowhere to be found, that's fer sure. Ain't nothin' no one kin do about that.'

Adela put the plates of eggs and bacon and mugs of coffee on the table in front of them.

'I'll do it,' Jack said. 'When I'm healed up, I'll start work on the mission. Maybe one of the cowboys from the Diamondback could help me, now the drive's left. Never thought I'd see myself a sheriff,' he added wryly.

'Folks will respect you. They'll trust you,' Blacklake said. 'That's what you need to be sheriff.'

'You can stay here until the mission house is fixed up,' Adela said.

'Well, damn. Ain't this somethin'?' Blacklake grinned. Adela sat down at the table beside them wreathed in smiles. All three raised their mugs of coffee in a toast to the future.

EPILOGUE

ONE YEAR LATER

Charlie was at the top of a ladder, with a hammer in his hand and a mouthful of nails. He had just fixed one end of a long white banner to the wooden wall of the saloon, directly above the door. When he was sure it was secure, he climbed down and leant his ladder up against the wall of the sheriff's office across the street, bringing the other end of the banner with him. Jack stepped out of the office and asked if he needed a hand.

'Nope. I'm fine,' Charlie called down cheerfully. He finished his work and climbed carefully down.

The two men walked down the street a few yards to see how it looked. The white sailcloth shone against the bright spring sky. The words 'Good Luck Boys! Diamondback Ranch 8th Spring Drive. Bigger and Better Every Year!' were painted in tall red letters across the width of the street.

'Looks fine, don't it?' Charlie said.

'Sure does,' Jack agreed. 'This your idea?'

'Yup. Wanted to make it sound real friendly. That's how come I put 'Good Luck Boys'. Took me a while to figure out what words to put.'

'Blacklake'll like that "Bigger and Better Every Year" part,' Jack said.

'Figured if I put that in, he might give me a raise.' Charlie grinned.

'You might be just about to find out.' Jack nodded towards a buggy which was approaching at a brisk trot. Blacklake was driving Adela.

Blacklake reined in the horses sharply and stared up at the sign. 'Well, I'll be. . . .' he began.

'It's to wish good luck to the boys,' Charlie explained.

'It's the finest piece of letterin' I ever saw.' Blacklake laughed. 'Outside of a column of figures in one of my account books, of course.'

'Good morning, Sheriff,' Adela called. 'It's a fine morning.'

' 'Mornin', Adela. It's good to see you out. Y'know, I still can't get used to you not wearing your eyeglasses.'

'I only wear them for reading now, Jack. I can't tell you how good the world looks. And for the first time in my life, I can see that I'm surrounded by all these handsome men!' Jack grinned and Charlie stared at his feet with embarrassment.

Adela stepped down out of the buggy and reached behind the seat for a basket. 'I've got something for you, anyhow. I was up early this morning and since it isn't a school day, I baked you one of my apple pies.'

'That's mighty nice of you, Adela. I'm makin' good progress on gettin' the mission homestead back together. But when it comes to cookin', I'm still on hard tack and beef jerky.'

'Well, at least today you'll have apple pie as well.'

Blacklake was still staring proudly up at the sign. 'Now Charlie, there's somethin' I've been meaning to talk to you about. Let's step into the saloon for a minute.'

Jack and Adela turned towards the sheriff's office. Inside, Adela carefully placed the pie, covered in its gingham napkin, in the centre of Jack's tidy desk.

'Y'know, I got the two Johnson boys workin' for me out at the mission now,' Jack said. 'I ain't got time for all the repair work needs doin'.'

'Well, you be careful with those two, after what they did to Clem.'

'They're just like anybody else, I reckon. Treat 'em right and they'll be good to you. Treat 'em mean, an' that's how they'll turn out.'

'I'm not sure Clem would agree with that,' Adela said cautiously.

'He's a fair-minded man,' Jack said. 'He'd see the sense in it.'

Adela smiled. 'If you say so, Sheriff. You're a fair-minded man yourself. Just what this town needs.'

The delicate scent of sugar and cloves had filled the office.

'Boy,' Jack said, 'that pie smells good. Reckon I might have to make a start on it right away. Let's cut it up and share it round. You'll have a piece, won't you, Adela? I know Charlie and your brother will want one.'

Later, Jack sat at his desk in the sheriff's office musing over how things had turned out. Only a year ago he'd been a saddle-sore drifter whose possessions amounted to a mule and a bag of carpenter's tools. Now he was the popular sheriff of a booming cattle town. He owned his own place; he earned a regular salary; his boss respected him and he had good friends in Clem and Charlie. But, gradually, over the long months, he had come to realize that none of this would have meant as much as it did if Adela had not been there.

He opened his desk drawer and took out a small blue box. He opened it and looked at the ring. Light flashed off the diamond. He had bought it from a salesman who had passed through from Kansas the previous week.

He'd faced tough situations all his life, things which tested all his courage and resolve. He'd fought in the war, quelled saloon fights, faced down gunmen, stood up against injustice and even taken a bullet. But he was surprised to find that none of this shook his nerve as much as what he had decided to do next.

He thought of Adela's sweet smile, her gentle, kindly ways and how her eyes shone when she looked at him. If he was going to stay on here, he knew he only wanted to do it if she was his wife. He put the blue box in his pocket and stood up, inwardly mustering all the certainty and strength which made him a cowboy. He went outside and mounted up. He would ride straight out to the Diamondback and find her.